Under the Old Sycamore Tree

The Story of a Slave in Ancient Egypt

FriesenPress

Suite 300 - 990 Fort St
Victoria, BC, V8V 3K2
Canada

www.friesenpress.com

Copyright © 2019 by Majd Khalaf
First Edition — 2019

Translated by Nezar Shahin

ISBN
978-1-5255-3988-6 (Hardcover)
978-1-5255-3989-3 (Paperback)
978-1-5255-3990-9 (eBook)

1. FICTION, HISTORICAL, ANCIENT

Distributed to the trade by The Ingram Book Company

Under the Old Sycamore Tree

The Story of a Slave in Ancient Egypt

MAJD KHALAF
NEZAR SHAHIN

PREFACE

Across the centuries, mankind has demonstrated an immense love and obsession for gathering items, materials, property, or any other entity they can call their own. This crazed obsession has lead mankind to transform the lives of their fellow man into a possession. The reason for this is greed. Greed, which is supposed to be a natural trait, has been transformed into a plague. It has made humans into blind, material-loving creatures who only strive to acquire more possessions even if they are the lives of their fellow man.

This book depicts the legend of Qaroon, an Israelite who lived just before the time of the liberation of the people of Israel. He was a slave who refused to submit to the Egyptians and rebelled against the fate of his people to rise up and become one of the wealthiest and most powerful men of his time. It is said that he resented his people and had a hand in their torture. He was so wealthy that the keys to his safes made even the strongest men struggle to carry them. Many people wondered how Qaroon achieved all this—whether it was due to sorcery, witchcraft, politics, alliances with the Pharaoh, pure genius, or a combination of all. This novel is an attempt to describe the methods by which Qaroon gathered his limitless fortune.

As it turns out, Ancient Egypt is not very different from modern countries today. This is evident in the way they are governed—how people flatter a ruler, how a ruler controls and oppresses people, how greed, hypocrisy and corruption raise a person to power, and how people like Qaroon can still exist in the world today

The enslavement of the people of Israel by the Egyptians around 33 centuries ago remains one of the most brutal and inhumane acts of violence ever inflicted on mankind. The Egyptians enslaved them, tortured them, raped their women and daughters, slaughtered their newborns, and robbed them of their freedom. This injustice will forever remain in history to serve as a lesson for us and a reminder that, when the opportunity presents itself, people take advantage of each other and enslave their fellow man to further their own power and influence.

CHAPTER 1

"WE ARE NOT EGYPTIANS; AND WE NEVER WILL BE."

The lands on the borders of the village of Goshen were all green, with many herbs and bushes. Two herdsmen, a father and his son, were walking together among their sheep and goats. The father was wearing dirty rags with a leather belt around his waist and an old white headband. His son was dressed similarly, but without the waist belt. Both of them had long staves to beat the branches for their sheep and goats.

"Qaroon, go get Pharaoh before he gets us into trouble again," Izhar said. He pointed at a big ram that was running towards a nearby cornfield. The boy ran to get the ram while his father walked tiredly to the shades of an old sycamore tree. He sat down on the ground and watched his son come back with the ram.

"Stay with your brothers, damned Pharaoh! Don't get us into trouble," Qaroon shouted at the ram. He gave it a light tap with his staff. "If you weren't so fluffy, you would've been served at the dinner table long ago." The ram obeyed and ran back to the herd. The boy then returned to his father beneath the tree.

"What kind of trouble are you afraid of, father?"

"The man that owns these lands will do anything to protect his crops. We can't have fat rams like Pharaoh running off and feasting on them."

"And why don't we own land?"

"The landlord is Egyptian. We are not. Simple as that."

The boy was silent for a few moments. "Where is our home-land, father? Or do we not have one?"

"I'm surprised Father Lawi hasn't spoken to you about this. He normally loves to preach about us eventually going back there."

"I would ask him, but he pinches my ear when I ask him anything."

Izhar laughed. "What is it with preachers and ear grabbing? My preacher used to do the same thing when I was young." He took a deep breath and sighed. "Our homeland is thirty days beyond that horizon," he said, pointing east.

"Why don't we go back there? Maybe back there we can own lands the same way the Egyptians do."

"We can't. We were born slaves, Qaroon. We belong to the Egyptians. If you owned a cow, you can't have it running off. The same applies to us. The Egyptians simply won't let us leave or go back there," he in a sad tone. "We were born here, and I'm afraid we're going to die here."

"Why did we even come here in the first place?" Qaroon asked.

"We have lived here ever since our ancestors, the sons of the Prophet Jacob, came to Egypt."

"That's the story that Father Lawi told us last week, but I didn't understand who the Hyksos were."

"The Hyksos were the rulers of Egypt when our ancestors came here. They had invaded northern Egypt some time ago. Those were our people's golden years, back when we owned lands. We were rich and proud. But when the Egyptians conquered the Hyksos and took back the throne of Egypt, they enslaved our people, humiliated them, seized their lands and riches, and forced them into slavery. That's how things have been for the last three hundred years. We can't go back because we are trapped here as their slaves. If we so much as try to cross the border, they will cut our heads off."

"But why do they treat us like this? What did we do?"

"They said we were supporting the Hyksos and were considered backstabbers and a threat to them."

"Were we supporting the Hyksos?" asked Qaroon.

"Of course, we were. If someone offers you lands and riches, you give them your full support. Enough questions for now, Qaroon! Go get us something to eat."

Qaroon stood up and walked to the tree, where he was hiding a bundle. In it was a piece of old cheese and some dry bread.

"I'm going to get us some onions," said Qaroon.

He ran near the field and picked onions from some dried up plants. He then ran back to his father and they started eating. Izhar noticed that his son was distracted.

"Is something bothering you?" Izhar asked.

"Now that I think about it, I don't want to go back to our home land. I'd rather stay here."

"It's not like you had the option of going back anyway." Izhar laughed.

"Father Lawi never shuts up about the promised deliverer who is supposed to lead our people out of slavery. I don't think that's true, but even if it was, I've decided I'd rather stay in Egypt."

"Why do you like Egypt so much?"

"Maybe one day we can be like the Egyptians and own a big piece of land like this," Qaroon said, pointing to the cornfield that spanned the entire area. "But if we leave, we never will."

Izhar smiled and didn't comment, but kept eating dry cheese and bread.

"Can we go to Memphis?" Qaroon asked.

"Are you mad? If the Egyptians figure out that we are from Israel, they will torture and kill us. No slave is allowed there without an Egyptian master. Maybe one day, you can get sold to an Egyptian who lives in Memphis." Izhar laughed again. "But why Memphis?"

"I wish to see its houses, streets, temples, and obelisks. I wish to see the Nile in the days of the flood."

"Your wishes are going to get us killed."

"If your fear is us being recognized, then we can go there in disguise. If we dress like them, nobody will know that we are from Israel."

Izhar was silent for a few moments. "A disguise is a good idea. It's been a while since I've seen Memphis, almost twenty years."

Qaroon rolled his eyes. "Such a selfish man! You went there before and you'd rather I get sold to an Egyptian than you take me there yourself?" Qaroon smiled as he threw a piece of bread at his father.

"It's every father's dream to have his children sold to Egyptians. That way, they can travel and see places," Izhar said, laughing.

"How very considerate of you!" Qaroon smiled.

After they finished eating, they started walking home with their sheep and goats. As they entered Goshen, a young boy approached them.

"Qaroon, we're going to play near my house. Do you wanna come or are you gonna stay home again?"

"Sorry, Benjamin, I'm not in the mood today. I'll join you tomorrow," said Qaroon.

"If you say so," Benjamin said. He waved goodbye and ran off.

"Feeling tired?" Izhar asked.

"Not at all. It's just that playing with Benjamin and the other boys is boring. We used to do fun things like throw rocks at Father Lawi's house, but then he caught us one day and the fun was over."

"You have a strange meaning of the word 'fun'. Just like your father." Izhar smiled. I used to throw rocks at my mother-in-law's house before I married your mother. I wish I could still do that now."

Qaroon laughed.

Qaroon and his father arrived at their home, a hut built of mud bricks. It had one small window and a broken wooden door. Qaroon opened the sheep pen door beside the hut and guided the sheep and goats in with his staff. He closed the door and went into the hut. The hut was very simple inside. In the main room were two brick platforms on both sides, an old wooden table, and a mud-built wood burner. At the end of the main room was a door that led to the inner two rooms and a simple kitchen. When Qaroon entered the place, he found his father sitting on the floor with his mother and his two younger sisters. They were sitting around a short-legged round table, on which food was presented in stoneware plates. Qaroon sat down with them and started to eat. Qaroon's mother noticed that he was a bit distracted.

"What's wrong, Qaroon?"

"Nothing. I'm just thinking," Qaroon replied.

"He wants to go to Memphis," said Izhar.

The mother and her two daughters all looked at Qaroon with astonishment.

"Why Memphis? Are you looking for trouble? Do you wanna get killed?" asked Qaroon's mother with a worried tone.

"I had a deal with father and he promised to take me there. Right, Father?" He looked at his father.

"Right. We will go to Memphis in a few months maybe."

Qaroon's mother gave Izhar an angry look.

"Why are you looking at me like that?" asked Izhar.

A few months later, Izhar and Qaroon were riding on a wooden carriage pulled by two mules. Qaroon was looking around happily. Green fields stretched as far as the horizon, gardens and meadows were full of grapes, pomegranates, and figs, and farmers were working in their fields with their axes and hatchets. Bulls were pulling wooden ploughs, countless egrets followed farmers and picked worms from the soil, and dozens of pigeons flew above. Qaroon kept gazing at a hawk flying high in the clear blue sky. They spent half of the day on the road.

"When you see farmers plowing land, then we are getting closer to the Nile. We are now in Thoth, the month after the Nile flood area, when the land is ready for farming," Izhar said.

"So last month farmers weren't working?" Qaroon asked.

"Last month was Mesore. The flood water covered the land and filled all canals, so there wasn't really that much that they could do."

"Are we getting close to Memphis?" Qaroon asked.

"I'm not taking you to Memphis," Izhar replied.

"Why not?"

"Memphis is too far. Heliopolis is so much closer to Goshen and I need to get back there because I don't trust your uncle Jacob with my sheep."

Qaroon seemed disappointed.

"Don't worry, Qaroon! You'll love Heliopolis. It has the biggest market in the area. Almost as big as the Memphis marketplace. And we can see the pyramids and the sphinx from there."

"I'll drop you off here because I have to get back to Goshen before it gets dark. I can't have bandits robbing me," said the cart driver.

They jumped off the carriage and Izhar gave the driver a bag of wheat.

"When will we arrive at Heliopolis, Maimoun?" Izhar asked.

"If you walk down this road, you should be there by night."

With the sun ahead, they started walking on the dirt road on the path to Heliopolis.

Sometime later, they stopped at a reed hut on the side of the road. When they went in, Izhar took some clothes out of his leather bag and handed them to Qaroon.

"Change your clothes and put on this leather belt."

"How is this head cover worn?"

"Just get dressed first, then I'll show you."

After Qaroon changed, Izhar put an Egyptian head cover on Qaroon's head and another one on his own. Qaroon seemed happy with his Egyptian clothes.

They came out of the hut and the sun was going down. Farmers began to ride donkeys and pull their cattle behind as they headed home. As they approached the big city, camphor and berry trees were on both sides of the road. After a long walk, the Nile River appeared orange as the sun sank. They walked faster to reach Heliopolis before dark.

The walls at the gates of Heliopolis were very high. People were scattered along the road, walking between giant stone ram statues. Qaroon was dazzled by what he was witnessing for the first time.

"The last time I came here, these ram statues weren't here."

"Do the Egyptians worship these statues, father?" asked Qaroon.

"If they didn't, they wouldn't bother building them. Let's turn around the walls, away from the gates."

"Where are we going to spend the night?"

"We'll see when we reach the Nile."

They walked around the walls for some time until they found a reed hut at the corner of a field. Izhar searched the corners of the hut with a stick.

"For snakes and scorpions," he said. They both lay down on the ground and put their bags under their heads. Soon, Izhar fell asleep, while Qaroon stayed awake. He waited until he heard his father snoring, then he got up and stepped out of the hut. He walked carefully towards the Nile's bank. He sat down under a tree by the river and rested. The cold night breeze made him shiver. He kept gazing at the horizon in the dark until he fell asleep.

When Qaroon woke up at dawn, he didn't know how long he had slept. He heard men's voices getting closer. A boat came out from behind the reeds. The two men looked surprised to see Qaroon so close to the water. They rowed until they reached him and let the front of the boat hit in the mud.

"Boy! What do you think you're doing sitting this close to the water?" said the first man.

"Aren't you afraid?" asked the second man.

Qaroon did not reply and looked confused. The two men jumped out of the boat and approached him.

"He is not from here."

"No, I am from Memphis. I just fell asleep. What is there to be afraid of?" asked Qaroon.

"You fell asleep here? You're lucky to be alive, boy. This could have ended with you in the belly of a crocodile."

"Crocodiles? Can they actually reach me here?"

"He is definitely not from here," the first man said, looking at the second man. "Don't you know that we are in Thoth? The Nile flood brings us water, but it also brings swarms of crocodiles."

"And you are not afraid?"

"Of course we are. Just yesterday, a huge crocodile killed a boy your age. They only managed to recover his right arm," said the second man.

"Our fishing nets also got torn apart by crocodiles trying to steal our fish."

"Just stay away from the water! Especially at sunrise," the first man said in a disciplinary tone.

He turned to his friend and they left together. As soon as they left the shore, Qaroon stood up and ran to his father in the hut.

Izhar and Qaroon walked on the riverbank wearing their Egyptian clothes. The pyramids on the west side looked enormous behind the long scattered palm trees.

"I don't understand why they made these pyramids for the dead," Qaroon said.

"Not any dead, only great kings and Pharaohs are buried in pyramids," Izhar replied.

"That is one fancy way to die. We get buried with worms and bugs while they get buried with more gold than we can imagine."

"That's just how things are. We're almost at the marketplace. Remember, you are Egyptian! Don't get us into trouble."

"Don't worry, Father," Qaroon said dismissively.

They walked towards the marketplace. They wandered in the crowd and Qaroon could not believe it. He kept asking his father about everything he saw. The marketplace was crowded with merchants and peddlers. Some were selling tools, stoneware and pottery, while others offered jewelry, colored stones, copper, turquoise beetles, icons, and amulets. Some sold cloth and textiles. Wheat, lentils, corn and beans were being weighed in metal plates and packed in smaller bags. Fishermen sold their fish in every shape and size. Other peddlers sold wine and beer packed in colored glass bottles. In a wide corner of the marketplace, merchants offered tools for farming: wooden ploughs, sickles, weeders, axes, hatchets, millstones, and pickaxes. Around the corner were a dozen more merchants who sold cattle, sheep, mules, donkeys, and horses. Not far from them, a few merchants sold animal skins. The noisiest part of the market was by the blacksmith, who sold swords, daggers, spears, and bamboo sticks. A man by the blacksmith was trying out a leather whip, making a terrifying noise. The blacksmith was yelling at a customer while the blacksmith's apprentice was hammering a molten red sword.

The busiest part of the marketplace was the slave traders' corner. Dozens of slave traders yelled their lungs out trying to advertise their merchandise. One of them called out to Qaroon and his father as they were walking by.

"A slave from the Nile springs. He does the work of two cows, minus the milk! However, if milk is what you want, I have a pregnant slave in stock." The slave trader burst into a mocking laugh.

Others offered slaves that could lift horses or crush a man's skull with their hands. Qaroon didn't seem to notice any slaves in particular, but then one caught his eye. He held a stick in his hands and was wearing torn rags with multiple bruises on his body.

"So you like Bayek? He is our finest stick fighter. This legendary beast can best three men at once!" said the slave trader.

"Not right now, sorry," said Qaroon while walking away. He then turned to his father. "What's a stick fighter?"

"Egyptians have a sport that involves men fighting against each other with wooden sticks. It is so popular that they started making their slaves fight in their stead," replied Izhar.

"Then why would that man sell his champion?"

"Exactly! If you had a champion, you'd only sell them if they're old or if they get badly injured. He's most likely trying to rob you."

Qaroon was silent for a moment. "Can we buy one of these slaves someday?" he asked.

Izhar was surprised. "You want to buy a slave, Qaroon? Are you insane? Our people are slaves! We are slaves. Did you ever hear of a slave who owns a slave?"

"If the Egyptians can do it, then so can we."

"We are not Egyptians, and we never will be."

"I refuse to believe that," Qaroon said.

"Believe what you like, Qaroon. That doesn't change the way things really are"

"Three slaves for the price of two. Get them now while they're still young!" yelled a slave trader as they passed.

"Feast your eyes on Claw! The fiercest stick fighter you've ever laid your eyes on!" yelled another. "When I found him, he had already killed two lions and was in the process of ripping the head off of the third."

Qaroon looked at the merchant's stock and saw a massive man standing next to the merchant. The merchant wasn't fully exaggerating. The slave looked like he could rip a lion's head off. His arms were twice as thick as the slave trader's legs. The slave could kill his Egyptian master right there. He could simply crush his skull, should he choose to, but for some reason, he didn't. Qaroon looked into the eyes of the giant and saw defeat and submission. All his strength and might amounted to nothing when he stood next to the man who owned his life. Qaroon didn't want to end up like that slave, or any other. He thought to himself that power isn't in strength or size; true power comes in possessions. The more possessions a man owned, the more powerful that man becomes. "But how does one acquire such possessions?" Qaroon asked himself.

"No more daydreaming, Qaroon. Let's keep going," said Izhar. He pulled Qaroon from in front of the slave trader's tent.

The customers of the slave market stood around a wooden stage, where slaves were presented. The people in the crowd yelled their prices to try to win the auctioned slaves.

"You want to join them, don't you?" asked Izhar.

"Maybe one day, I will," replied Qaroon, with an ambitious look in his eyes.

Izhar sighed and looked at his son. "Listen to me, Qaroon. It's better to be where you are now then up on that stage getting sold to the highest bidder and having your dignity taken away from you."

"But it's also better to be the highest bidder and take people's dignities away than to be where I am right now," said Qaroon, as if challenging his father.

"We'll talk about this later," said Izhar. He looked disappointed.

Qaroon and Izhar walked towards a crowd that formed a circle around a magician. He stood in the middle of the circle playing with a stick. He threw it on the ground and the stick turned into a cobra. When he held the snake in his hands, it turned back into a stick.

Qaroon was shocked. "How is he doing that, Father?"

"I honestly don't know, but my father told me it was witchcraft and involved manipulating people's minds. But it's nonsense if you ask me. It's probably some cheap magic trick that he mastered."

"It doesn't look cheap."

They saw another circle around two slaves who were fighting with sticks. People kept cheering for both fighters until one of them struck the other in the face and knocked his teeth out. He fell to the ground and the crowd roared with excitement. Some were cheering and others walked away in disappointment.

"Well done, Anoob!" said a man as he patted the victorious slave on his back. "You win me two more fights today, and I promise not to feed you to the dogs. Win me three, and tonight I'll let you eat my leftovers."

The slave had blood on his face but Qaroon could still see the fear in his expression. Qaroon and his father resumed walking.

At the end of the marketplace, Qaroon and Izhar stopped at an old woman's wood burner. She was making pies. Izhar bought two pies and they walked until they sat down by one of the giant pillars of Amun's temple. They started eating their pies.

"It is a huge market. I have never seen anything like it," Qaroon said.

"In Barmahat, two months from now, the amount of people here doubles, so more traders show up," said Izhar.

"Because it is harvesting season?" he asked.

"Yes. There is no place in the world like Egypt, especially in Barmahat."

Izhar and Qaroon finished eating their pies and drank from a nearby water well. They walked towards the Nile bank. The sun was going down behind the horizon, which was stained with a clear orange color. Numerous seagulls and great herons were flying home in the sunset. The great pyramid rested in peace on the other side.

"Can we go there?" asked Qaroon while pointing at the pyramid.

"There is nothing there except graves and corpses."

"I wish to go there to see the pyramid while standing at its base."

"The whole west bank is guarded with armed soldiers."

"They're guarding corpses?" asked Qaroon.

"They're not guarding the corpses. but what is buried with them."

"The gold!" Qaroon nodded.

"Of course. That's why they have to guard them. Tomb raiders never stop trying to steal the treasures buried there."

"But why bother putting treasures and gold with corpses? They don't need them."

"They think they need them. Egyptians believe in another life after death. After stuffing the bodies of the dead, they place them in a tomb and fill the tombs with all the things they think the dead will need in their new life. They put gold, silver, masks, and statues. They even provide them with food, honey, wine, and bread," Izhar said, laughing.

"They put all that treasure there when it could be used elsewhere?"

"Elsewhere?" asked Izhar.

"For people like us, I mean."

"What would you do with such a fortune?" Izhar raised his eyebrows.

"First thing I would do is buy a farm and force Father Lawi to work in it." Qaroon laughed.

"You won't give anything to the people of Goshen?"

"Only if they come work on my farm."

"How very generous of you, Qaroon!" said Izhar.

"But those tomb raiders have the right idea."

"Don't get any ideas. Most of the time they are caught and executed. But yes, sometimes they escape. When the guards come to check the tombs in the morning, they find them opened and raided."

"Can we go to the pyramids so I can see one up close?"

"We'll try tomorrow, but now let's go back to the hut before it gets dark," said Izhar.

After some time, Izhar and Qaroon arrived back at the hut, placed their bags under their heads, and quickly fell asleep.

"Wake up. Who are you?" said a man's voice.

Izhar woke up to being poked with a stick.

"What are you doing in my hut?" said the man. He looked hostile.

Izhar looked around and Qaroon wasn't there. "I am a stranger who came here last night. I needed a place to sleep. What's wrong with that?"

"This isn't your hut to sleep in," shouted the man.

"So? I didn't break or steal anything. Would you rather that I sleep outside in the dirt?"

The man's face calmed down a bit. "My apologies. We were robbed not too long ago and I am just being cautious. Get up and go to wash your face in the Nile and come back to have some food."

Izhar stood up. "What is the generous man's name?"

"Helal. And what is the intruding man's name?" He smiled.

"Iz... Badri. My name is Badri. I'll be right back." Izhar walked out of the hut and made his way to the Nile. He was looking for Qaroon. He found him hiding behind a big tree.

"What did the man say?" asked Qaroon.

"He is a good man. He is offering us food. Remember, we are Egyptians! By the way, I told him my name is Badri, so you tell him that your name is Adham."

"What does it mean?"

"In Egyptian, 'Adham' means generous."

"You couldn't have described me better," said Qaroon, smiling.

They both washed their faces and walked back to the hut. They found Helal sitting on a mat in front of the hut. He had several pieces of old cheese, milk, cream, and fresh baked bread in front of him.

"Adham, say hello to Helal."

"Your son?" Helal said as he shook hands with Qaroon.

They sat down to eat with Helal.

"Where are you from, Badri?"

"We are from Memphis," replied Izhar.

"The best people."

"You are too kind," Izhar said, smiling.

"How many years has the Nile flood been high?" asked Qaroon.

"Maybe three or four years. Why do you ask?"

"And before that, was it lower or higher?"

"It was lower. Water didn't even reach the base of that tree over there, while in the past three years, as you can see, the water is up to the middle of the tree," replied Helal.

"Don't bother the man with all your questions, Adham!" said Izhar.

"It is no problem at all!" said Helal. "Do you have any other children, Badri?"

"Other than Adham, I have two girls."

"I have two boys and one girl. My second son, Minali, is just about your age, Adham."

"Maybe I can meet him one day," said Qaroon.

"I was honoured today with your presence, brother Badri. You too, Adham."

"The honour is all ours, brother Helal. You have been very kind to us. Someday we will repay your kindness. But we have to go home now."

"Next time you visit Heliopolis, please feel free to intrude on my hut," said Helal with a smile.

"We will!" Izhar laughed. "We surely will. Goodbye!"

"Goodbye. Safe travels," said Helal.

Qaroon and Izhar were off.

Before noon, they saw a small wooden sailboat heading towards their bank of the Nile. When it arrived, Izhar helped the boatman pulling the ropes and shifting the boat's rudder. Qaroon was eagerly watching the pyramids on the west bank.

"How much time will it take us to cross the Nile?" Izhar asked as he looked at the boatman.

"You are lucky because today the wind is with us. It shouldn't take that long to get to the other side. Why do you want to go there?"

"One of the guards is my brother. We are just bringing him some food for the next few days."

"How long are you going to stay there?"

"Not long at all. We will give him the bag and return right away."

"Try not to go near the pyramid entrances because that's where all the guards usually stand. It's better to be back before dusk."

"We will. Thank you!" said Izhar.

The wind blew strongly and the boat came closer to the west bank. Qaroon jumped off the boat the moment it hit the sandy ground and Izhar followed him.

"Please, don't leave without us!" Izhar said with a smile.

"I'll leave as soon as the sun starts to set. If you're back by then, good. If not, you'll have to manage," the boatman said. He sat down on a platform on his boat.

Izhar turned around and saw Qaroon rushing towards the pyramids, so he ran after him. When he caught up, he was panting.

"It's too far!" complained Qaroon.

"Let's walk faster so we can get there before noon. We need to find some shade before the sun burns us alive."

They walked in the sand with difficulty but tried to keep a steady pace.

"Isn't there another way?" asked Qaroon.

"There's another road to the north, but with a lot more guards. This way is better."

"It's funny how you're always asking me to stay out of trouble but here you are taking me to the pyramids"

"I told you not to get us into trouble, but I can do as I please," said Izhar.

"Hypocrite!"

They kept walking until at last, they were standing at the base of a pyramid. Qaroon stared at it in amazement. They sat to rest in the shadow of a broken temple pole.

"Why do they bury the dead here? I mean, why west?" asked Qaroon.

"I think because here the land is dry, so the dead bodies and mummies do not rot."

"How did they get those huge stones up there?"

"I don't know, but Egyptians are master architects. Plus, they have tens of thousands of slaves. I'm sure they must have managed with that."

"This is why we shouldn't be slaves. Egyptians get statues and pyramids that glorify them for eternity while slaves get whipped on the back after a long and exhausting day of lifting bricks," complained Qaroon.

"Go ahead then, son. Go buy yourself a few thousand slaves and build a statue of yourself," said Izhar.

Qaroon dismissed his father's mockery and looked at the other two nearby pyramids .

"Is the third pyramid as big as that one?" he asked, pointing.

"No, this is the biggest pyramid. Other pyramids are smaller. Even the ones built in Sakkarah and Meidum to the south are much smaller."

"Let's go back to catch the boatman before he leaves us here."

"This soon? We just got here."

"I wanted to come here to see the pyramids up close, and I did. There's no point in looking at it again. We still need to see the sphinx though."

"We'll pass it on the way back."

They started to walk back but headed towards the sphinx. Qaroon saw something shining buried in the sand and bent down to pick it up. It was a golden bracelet. He smiled and immediately hid it in his rags. He then continued walking in the deep sea of sand until they reached the sphinx. They sat in its shadow to eat some dates and bread.

"The statue is indeed amazing. It's not very humble, but still amazing; but the nose is too big," said Qaroon. "It looks like it might fall off."

"Maybe the Pharaoh who had this statue made had a really big nose."

They finished their food and then started walking back to the Nile. When they arrived, the boatman was preparing to go back.

"Perfect timing," he said.

They jumped on the boat and they sailed back. After reaching the other side of the Nile, the boatman sailed away.

"Let me see if I can manage to get someone with a cart to give us a ride to the borders of Goshen," said Izhar.

Later, the sky was illuminated by a full moon. Qaroon and his father were walking back to Goshen. Qaroon noticed that his father was a bit troubled.

"What's bothering you, Father?"

"Nothing. I'm just thinking about my herd. I'm worried your uncle Jacob has ended up feeding them poisonous herbs or accidentally driving them off a cliff."

"You worry too much!"

"I have every reason to worry. Goshen is in a terrible condition and I'm barely able to feed you, your mother, and your sisters. When the drought comes, we're all going to starve."

"Not really," said Qaroon. He took the bracelet out from his pocket. Izhar's eyes sparkled with joy when he saw the gold and he smiled.

"Where did you get this?" He took it in his hand. "It's heavy. Did you steal it?"

"No, I found it in the sand while we were walking between the pyramids and the sphinx."

"One of those tomb raiders must have dropped it while escaping." Izhar stared at the bracelet for a few moments. "This bracelet is..."

"This bracelet is going to stay with me!" Qaroon interrupted. He took the bracelet from his father's hand. "And you're going to sell half of your sheep and give me the money."

"Sell the sheep? Are you mad?" yelled Izhar.

"Am I mad for wanting my father to be the wealthiest man in Israel?"

"Me? Ha!" said Izhar with a laugh. "The wealthiest man in Israel? It seems that today's hot sun has fried your greedy brain."

"I'm not mad. This amulet is more than enough to help me in what I'm planning. I'm just asking you to sell the sheep so you can contribute and be my partner. Just do what I say and you'll see. Trust me!"

"Trust you? You're still young and you know nothing about how the world works"

"And you do?"

"More than you, Qaroon."

"Just trust me, Father. The worst case scenario is you will have to rebuy the sheep that you sold. But that's not going to happen because I know what I'm thinking will work."

"How can you be so sure about that?" asked Izhar.

"I'll tell you later. Right now, I just want to go home and sleep."

They didn't speak until they entered their house in Goshen. Izhar went to check on his sheep and Qaroon immediately rushed to bed.

The next morning, Qaroon woke up to the sound of his mother calling.

"Qaroon! Wake up! Have your breakfast before you go with your father. Before you feed the sheep, feed yourself!"

Qaroon got up and quickly checked his rags. He smiled and took the amulet out. He then hid it somewhere in the room and walked out to have breakfast with his family. His two sisters and his mother were all sitting around the small wooden table. Izhar walked in from outside.

"Good morning, Pharaoh! How many statues of yourself have you built today?" Izhar asked with a smile.

Qaroon dismissed his father's mockery and sat down to eat.

"Your father told us about your dreams of owning slaves," Qaroon's mother said. She smiled and shook her head.

"It's not just about owning slaves. It's about having anything an Egyptian has. It's about being their equal."

"I doubt that's going to happen anytime soon," Izhar said as he sat down.

"Father, I heard some soldiers are coming today to take some men for a new temple that they're building," said Rebecca.

"Again?" Qaroon's mother rolled her eyes. "Tens of thousands of slaves aren't enough?"

"Many of them die every day, so they need to replace them," replied Izhar. "Let's just hope they don't take me or Qaroon."

"Which one of you two girls would like to go and refill the water buckets? Leah?" asked Qaroon's mother.

"Sure thing," replied Leah.

"Qaroon, why don't you go with her?" asked Izhar. "Give her a hand and make sure she doesn't break any of the buckets."

"But we're going to be late for the sheep herding," said Qaroon.

"You're right. You go with your sister and I'll bring the sheep and meet you there. We'll take as much water as we need and then we'll head over to the herb lands."

"Sounds good."

Qaroon and his sister Leah walked out of the hut. They grabbed one bucket each and headed towards the water well, which was a rather long walk from Goshen.

"I hate how far the water well is from the village," Qaroon complained.

"You're not the one who has to walk back with the buckets, so stop complaining."

After walking for a while, from a distance, they saw a horse chariot by the water well. Some men were standing there. It was clear they were the Egyptian soldiers who were to take a few men from Goshen.

"We should turn back before they see us," said Leah.

When they turned around to leave, they saw an Egyptian soldier standing behind them.

"Going somewhere?" asked the Egyptian with a smile.

"We were just getting some water," said Qaroon.

The soldier whistled loudly and the other soldiers rushed to where he was.

"Looks like we're going to have some fun, boys!" one of the Egyptians said with a smile.

"I get this one," said another soldier.

"You got the last one! It's my turn!"

"Fine, you can have this one. There's plenty of other slaves for me in the village."

"One of the soldiers grabbed Leah. She dropped the bucket and started to scream.

"Let go of my sister!" Qaroon shouted. He rushed towards the Egyptian who grabbed her.

Two of the soldiers grabbed Qaroon's arms and he couldn't move.

"Manners! Is this how you treat your masters?"

Leah continued to scream as the Egyptian started ripping off her rags from the bottom.

"No! Please no!" Qaroon pleaded. "Let her go, please!" He started to cry.

Leah's screaming grew louder so the soldier hit her face.

"Shut up, you dirty whore!"

"You need to be taught some manners!" one soldier said to Qaroon as he removed a whip from his belt. "Turn him around. He doesn't have to see this."

The soldiers turned Qaroon around to face the village. Leah was now screaming in pain and crying.

"Please! Stop hurting her!" Qaroon cried. "Plea..."

Before he could continue his sentence, he felt the whip strike his back. It felt as if he had been electrocuted. Qaroon screamed in pain. He felt helpless. He couldn't save his sister and he couldn't fight back. He let out another cry when a second lash of the whip struck his back, tearing his clothes and letting out blood. Leah's screams were muffled as the Egyptian put his hand on her mouth. Qaroon was looking at the ground and shaking. He raised his head to see something he had not expected. He saw his father standing at a distance with the herd of sheep and goats behind him.

"Father!" Qaroon cried. "Father, help!"

Izhar remained still and watched as his daughter was raped and his son whipped.

"Father, please!" Qaroon cried. A tear rushed down his cheek. "We need you!"

"Shut up, you little shit! Learn to fear your masters! Your father is doing a good job," the soldier whipping him said. He struck Qaroon again.

Izhar did nothing. He simply froze in his place.

"Boys! His back is full of wounds. We wouldn't want him to get any infections, would we?" one of the soldiers said. He motioned another to run to the chariot. "Don't worry, boy! We're going to close all of your wounds so they don't get infected."

Qaroon was shivering and his head was facing the ground. A soldier returned from the chariot with a lit torch. He passed it to the one who was whipping Qaroon.

The soldier who was raping Leah got off of her. She was whimpering. He then walked over to Qaroon.

"Is your mother as pretty as your sister?" he asked, smiling. "If so, you need to take me to her." He laughed.

Qaroon couldn't speak. He just raised his head and looked into the eyes of the man who raped his sister. He gave him a look of hate and despise. The soldier punched Qaroon in the face.

"That is no way to look at your superior, slave!"

Leah was still on the ground crying and Izhar was watching at a distance.

"I like his spirit," said one of the soldiers. "Maybe one day he can help build a temple or two before his spine is broken. Close his wounds!"

Qaroon felt heat near his back.

"We don't want to burn him. Take his rags off!"

With one move, one of the soldiers ripped Qaroon's rags off, exposing his bleeding back with multiple open wounds.

Qaroon felt heat approaching his back again. He started to scream when the flame touched his open wounds. The soldiers laughed as he screamed. He was about to pass out from the pain. The last thing he saw before blacking out was his father standing at a distance.

Some time passed.

"Qaroon!"

He was being shaken.

"Qaroon, wake up!"

He opened his eyes to find his father kneeling over him and his sister crying in the back, covered with her torn clothes. He felt the burn marks on his back and looked at his father.

"Why?" he asked angrily. "Why?" A tear escaped his eye. "Why didn't you help us?"

Izhar teared up. "I'm so sorry, Qaroon!"

"What kind of father are you? What kind of man are you? You let your own daughter get raped and your son get whipped and burned. And you just watched? What kind of man are you?"

"What could I have done, Qaroon? They would have killed me and continue hurting you."

"Better die trying than just watch."

"If I die, who will feed the family? Qaroon, I'm so sorry this happened, but this is how things are. This has happened before to others and it will keep happening. You just have to accept it."

"I have to accept it? I have to accept this? What kind of life is this? What kind of person can live like this? Not even an animal would accept this kind of life."

"There is nothing that can be done about it."

Qaroon stood up and started walking back to Goshen.

CHAPTER 2

"I'M NOT GOING TO DIE A SLAVE."

A month later, Qaroon and Benjamin were on their way to Father Lawi's house one morning for their weekly religious lectures. On their way, they were kicking a ball made of straw and palm tree leaves to each other. When the ball was kicked, it created a trail of dust where it landed. Qaroon kicked it to Benjamin.

"What are we even doing? I'm bored!" Qaroon complained.

"What do you mean you're bored? We do this all the time!" replied Benjamin.

"Exactly! What's the fun in doing the same exact thing every day, or eating the same meal every day?"

"There's really not much we can do about it. We'll just keep doing the exact same thing our ancestors did until we die. It's who we are."

"No! I am not like you! I refuse to die like the rest of you."

"Do you think you're any different from the rest of us? We're all slaves here, Qaroon. We're all dirt in the eyes of the Egyptians. What makes you any special?"

"I'm not accepting my fate like the rest of you. I'm not going to die a slave!"

"How are you going to escape your destiny? You're destined to be a slave. Just like the rest of us!"

Qaroon sighed. "This is the fault of our ancestors! Why do we have to suffer their mistakes?"

"What could they have done?"

"They could have done something about it, but they didn't. They chose to remain silent while they got whipped. They chose to remain silent while their kids were slaughtered and their wives and daughters raped. They chose to remain silent when they were forced into centuries of slavery. The worst part is, they taught their helplessness to their children so they were also born with no pride or spirit. You want me to accept my fate? Accepting their fate is what got them and us into this in the first place! This is why I don't consider myself one of you, because you refuse to act. You just sit down and accept whatever knife stabs you in the heart."

Benjamin did not reply. When Qaroon passed the ball to him, he kicked it hard and it went flying into the cornfield on the side of the dirt road. Benjamin panicked and ran after the ball immediately, before it was too late. But it was! As he was about to enter the field, an Egyptian farmer with a large axe over his shoulder emerged from the field.

"Where do you think you're going, you son of a whore?" the farmer shouted.

Benjamin froze. "Uhm… No where… I was just… getting my ball," Benjamin said, terrified.

"If you so much as lay a hand on my crops, I'll chop your arm off with my axe and feed it to my dogs."

"What did he ever do to you, you filthy pig?" Qaroon shouted at the farmer.

"I'm a pig? You forget who you're speaking to, slave! Both of you, get off my land or I will burn your slave village to the ground."

"You're a…" Qaroon started shouting but was interrupted.

"We'll be on our way. But could you please do us a favor and give us our ball back?"

"You're not getting anything from me! Now, get off my land before I take your other two balls," shouted the farmer. He put the axe over his other shoulder. He then got down and started to throw rocks at them.

The two boys quickly retreated and went to stand under a nearby tree.

"I'll get you your ball back, Benjamin!"

"How? I don't think he was joking about chopping our arms or balls off or burning down the village."

"You'll see. Follow me!"

Qaroon started to walk around the field and Benjamin followed.

"What're you up to, Qaroon? Don't get us into trouble. I can just make another ball, but I can't grow another pair if he cuts my balls off," Benjamin complained.

Qaroon did not reply.

They continued walking until they reached the other end of the field. Qaroon went into the field first and Benjamin followed. They quietly navigated through the field until the man appeared in front of them. He was sitting down in front of a fire and had his two donkeys tied to a nearby tree.

"You stay here! I'm going to sneak up behind him and look for the ball. When you see me on the other side, make a sound to distract him," Qaroon whispered.

"What kind of sound?"

Qaroon didn't reply but snuck into the cornfield.

"Qaroon!" Benjamin whispered loudly.

A short while later, Qaroon's face emerged from field on the other side. Qaroon then signaled to Benjamin, who hesitated for a few seconds but then let out an awkward howl.

"What kind of retarded wolf are you?" yelled the farmer. He grabbed his axe and got up. He started walking towards Benjamin.

Qaroon quietly got out of hiding and walked towards the farmer. When he got closer, he grabbed a large rock that was on the ground. The farmer was still searching for the source of the noise in the field. Qaroon got closer to the farmer because the rock was too heavy to throw at a distance. As soon as he was close enough, he threw the rock at the farmer's head. The farmer screamed in pain, dropped his axe, and fell to the ground

"Qaroon! What did you just do?" shouted Benjamin.

"Qaroon, is it?" asked the farmer, who was now on the ground lying on his back with his head bleeding. The farmer raised his head off the ground. "You're dead, Qaroon! You and every member of your family! I will kill all of you and feed your corpses to my dogs."

Qaroon did not say anything, but slowly bent down and grabbed the farmer's axe.

"What do you think you're doing, slave? Put that axe down!"

Qaroon was standing right next to the farmer, who was still lying on his back. He didn't move because Qaroon could easily strike him down with the axe.

Benjamin came out of the cornfield. "Qaroon, put the axe down! Let's go!"

"Listen to your friend, you worthless bastard!" said the farmer. He looked into Qaroon's eyes with a hateful look while blood was running down his face.

Qaroon remained silent, just looking at the man who was now at his mercy.

"Qaroon?" asked Benjamin in a faint tone.

"You're pathetic! You're worthless! My donkey is worth more than you! One donkey of mine is worth more than you and all of your kind!" The man started to shout.

"I'm worth more than your rotting corpse!"

The farmer's eyes widened in horror as he saw Qaroon swing the axe above his shoulder.

"You filthy..." The farmer was interrupted by the axe penetrating his left rib cage. He gasped for air and his body started shaking. Moments later, blood started flowing out of his mouth. He looked into the eyes of his killer and saw hate. Pure hate! No remorse and certainly no regret. The farmer returned the hateful look and uttered, "S... SS ...Slave!" He spat out blood with his final word. He then exhaled and his head fell to the side. Qaroon let go of the axe and started panting.

Benjamin stood there in horror and watched the blood flow out of the farmer.

"Qaroon! You... You killed him!"

"He deserved it."

"No one deserves to die over a ball!" Benjamin yelled.

"You think I killed him for a ball? You moron! No matter how humiliated you get, you just swallow it. You were willing to let this animal insult you like that and you were just going to walk away! This is why I am not like you! I refuse to be a slave like the rest of you. What I did should have happened centuries ago, back when this all started."

"It's too late now! Shaming you for what you did won't change anything. We'd better go!"

The two boys rushed out of the field and were back on their path to Father Lawi's house.

"You don't tell a soul what happened!" Qaroon said sternly.

"Are you mad? Why would I tell anyone? I'll just get in trouble for helping you."

"Just remember, I did this for you."

"You did this for me?" Benjamin said in a mocking tone. "I didn't want you to kill the man."

"He insulted both of us and was threatening to kill us and burn down the village. I don't even think he was joking about that last part."

"You killed him because you wanted to, Qaroon! You didn't do it for me or for Goshen."

"Let's walk faster or we'll be late and Father Lawi will give us a useless lecture on discipline."

Like any other house in Goshen, Father Lawi's house showed signs of poverty. It was made of mud and smelled of shit due to the nearby farm animals. When Qaroon and Benjamin stepped in to the house, they saw the dozens of children who had made their way before them. Father Lawi stopped preaching when he saw the two of them enter. He gave both of them an angry look and started to walk towards them. He was an older man with a long, full beard covering most of his face. He wore rags just like everyone else. His back was slightly hunched but it was masked in the eyes of the observer because Father Lawi was rather tall compared to the rest of the villagers in Goshen. As soon as he reached them, he grabbed both of them by the ear.

"Where have you two been?"

"We were walking fast to get here, Father Lawi. We're sorry!" said Benjamin.

"I'm not!" said Qaroon in a neutral tone.

"You're not sorry?" Father Lawi asked, pinching his ear harder.

"Why should I be?" Qaroon said as he slipped from Father Lawi's grasp and took a step back. "Why should I be sorry?" he repeated. "I come here every week and listen to the same preachings. I'm bored of you, Father Lawi. You're a boring man, and your God isn't any less boring than you are!"

"What did you just say? Blasphemy! First, you insult your preacher, and then you insult your God? He will punish you for this, Qaroon," Father Lawi shouted.

"The same way he's punishing the Egyptians? Those non-believers who you've been praying for your God to strike down your entire life?"

"These are the words of a non-believer! Blasphemous child, withdraw your foul tongue, or God almighty shall strike you down!" Father Lawi shouted at Qaroon and gave him angry looks.

"You and thousands of Israelites have been praying for salvation from slavery for centuries. If your God truly existed, then why does he let the so-called believers like you rot in Goshen?"

"Get out! This is a place of God! This is not a place for blasphemous and damned devil worshippers like you!"

"Father Lawi, how can I live without your marvellous preachings?" Qaroon said sarcastically as he retreated backwards out of the door.

"Your father will hear about this, Qaroon!" Father Lawi shouted loudly.

Qaroon exited the house and Father Lawi gave Benjamin a spiteful look.

"You too!" said Father Lawi.

Benjamin quickly retreated in fear and ran to catch up with Qaroon.

"You're rebellious lately, Qaroon! What is wrong with you?"

"Nothing is wrong with me. I'm just starting to see things for how they really are, not those filthy lies that we've been fed our whole lives."

"What filthy lies? You mean Father Lawi?" asked Benjamin.

"Not just him, but everyone! The idea that getting enslaved was the Egyptians' fault and not ours. The belief that there's nothing we can do. The fact that we worship an invisible man in the sky. The myths of a deliverer, one man that will supposedly free us from slavery."

"But what if this deliverer does come?"

"The only way he appears is if he takes advantage of the opportunity and claims to be a deliverer just so he can rule the Israelites. That would be the smart thing to do."

Benjamin sighed, but before he could reply, they heard a girl crying on their way back. It was at the field where Qaroon had killed the Egyptian farmer.

"Father…" cried the girl. "Who could have done this to you?"

"Let's get out of here, Qaroon!"

"No, wait!" Qaroon walked towards the field. "Let's go take a look." He ran through the field.

"Qaroon!" Benjamin whispered loudly. There was no reply so Benjamin followed him through the field. He walked towards where Qaroon had killed the farmer and he found his friend hiding in the field. In front of them was a girl on her knees in front of the farmer's still bleeding corpse, crying.

"That is one beautiful girl," said Qaroon, smiling.

"Have you lost your mind?" whispered Benjamin angrily. "You just killed her father! Wipe that smile off your face and let's go!" Benjamin grabbed Qaroon by the arm and pulled him back. They got back on the path back to Goshen.

Later, Qaroon was sitting on the floor with his sisters around a table. There were plates and wooden spoons in front of them and their mother was preparing food in a large pot.

Qaroon touched his back and felt pain in his scars. He remembered the whipping and the burning sensation. He then looked at his sister Leah, who appeared to be fine.

"How can she be fine?" Qaroon asked himself. "Did she forget what happened? Was it not traumatizing for her? Was it not humiliating? How can she just forget? Maybe she is just pretending to be fine." He then looked at his mother, who also seemed fine. "Why is no one mad? Why is no one scarred?"

"I'm back!" said Izhar as he walked in.

"Dinner is just about ready!" said his wife.

Izhar took a seat between Qaroon and Rebecca.

Qaroon looked at his father, who also appeared to be fine. "Why is he not mad? Why is he not furious? Why has he dismissed the incident? What kind of father can watch his children get tortured and continue to live normally? Is it so normal that it is easily forgotten? How can he sleep at night? How can any Israelite live and breathe every day in this humiliating life? Why is no one doing anything about it?" Qaroon was furious but concealed his anger.

"What's wrong, father? You look troubled," asked Rebecca.

Izhar sighed. "Joshua's son, Azir, is dead."

With exception of Qaroon, the family looked at Izhar in shock.

"God of Abraham! He's so young," said Izhar's wife.

"He just got married, the poor man," said Rebecca.

"How did he die?" asked Leah.

"The man had a problem with his temper. He was working today at an Egyptian's farm. Just normal everyday work! He was cleaning out the man's cattle stable. He was moving leftover hay from inside the stable to the outside. The Egyptian was sitting nearby eating and Azir accidentally dropped some of the hay on him."

"The Egyptian killed him over that?" Izhar's wife asked.

"Let me finish! The Egyptian then got up and hit him in the face and called him and his family names. Azir lost his temper and threw all of the dirty leftover hay on him. This gave the Egyptian every excuse to gut Azir open with a knife."

Qaroon laughed.

"You think this is funny, Qaroon?" Izhar gave his son a stern look.

"Of course it's funny! It's funny how stuff like this happens to us every day and we're just sitting down peacefully and eating. An Israelite getting gutted by an Egyptian is so normal to us that we're just going to hear the story, feel pity for the victim, curse the Egyptians, pray to God to save us, and then forget about it the next day."

"What would you have us do?" asked Izhar.

"Why would God do something for us if we're not going to bother doing it ourselves? Where's the logic in that? By that logic, every single man who ever prayed would be the richest man alive because they pray so much."

"So you want us to go and kill the Egyptians?" asked Izhar in a mocking tone.

"See? This is the problem! No one wants to do anything about anything. Instead of praying to a God for help, why not grab a knife and go gut the man who gutted one of ours?"

"Because we'll only end up getting ourselves gutted as well," said Izhar.

"If that's what it takes to get rid of these Egyptians, then so be it."

"No son of mine will go marching towards Egyptians with a knife! I won't allow it! You'll only get yourself killed and make Goshen suffer because of the Egyptians' wrath."

"You misunderstood me, Father. I'm not going to do anything! This is your problem. I will not suffer the consequences of my cowardly ancestors."

"Whether you like it or not, Qaroon, you are one of us. Our fate is yours."

Qaroon's mother served the food in front of her family and then took a seat. The family was silent for sometime.

"I heard that the Egyptian that owns the nearby cornfields was killed today," said Rebecca. "They say his daughter found him with an axe in his chest."

"Well deserved!" Qaroon said.

"Indeed!" said Izhar. "But they will most likely blame Goshen for this."

"Do you mean the cornfield on the way to Father Lawi's house?" asked Leah.

"Yes, that's the one!" replied Izhar. "Speaking of Father Lawi..." Izhar turned to Qaroon. "Care to explain why the man kicked you out of his house and called you a blasphemous non-believer?"

"I only told him things that he already knows but refuses to admit," said Qaroon before taking a bite out of a piece of bread.

"He's the most holy man in Goshen! He knows more than any of us!" said Qaroon's mother.

"What exactly does Father Lawi know?" Qaroon asked. "Father Lawi has the potential to motivate Israelites to resist slavery, but instead he just tells us to put our hands out and beg God for help. Like I said, God will not do something for us if we won't even bother doing it ourselves."

"According to Father Lawi, you don't even think that God exists," said Izhar.

"Can you blame me? Centuries of praying for salvation from slavery, and God does nothing. All he does is promise to send us a deliverer to free us! One man, an Israelite, against the whole of Egypt, against the might of Pharaoh!"

"The boy has completely lost faith, Izhar!" complained Qaroon's mother.

"Once the deliverer comes, he will return to his faith and repent. Won't you, Qaroon?"

"If you say so, Father."

The next morning, Qaroon woke up to the sound of the wooden door of their hut being broken down. Four Egyptian soldiers came rushing in, grabbed Izhar, and started to take him out of the hut.

"Qaroon! The herd is your responsibility!" shouted Izhar. "Don't lose any of them!"

The soldiers took Izhar into a line of many of the men of Goshen. They were investigating the murder of the Egyptian farmer. The soldiers tied all the men they apprehended by the hand and started to drag them along the path outside of Goshen.

For the next few days, Qaroon watched his father's herd near the dead Egyptian's cornfields. He would go to that area because he was able to see the dead farmer's daughter on her way to and from the cornfield. Every morning, she would go to the cornfield riding a donkey and pulling a cow behind her. Despite the grief on her face, Qaroon admired her beauty. She was almost the same age as him, with black hair that would swing behind her while she was riding the donkey.

One morning, Qaroon woke up early and did not take the sheep with him. His father had not returned yet. He went over to where he knew the girl would be. She was resting under a tree near the cornfield on her father's land. Qaroon snuck up from behind.

"Lovely day, isn't it?" asked Qaroon.

The girl immediately got up, frightened, and looked at Qaroon. "This is my father's land! If you have no business here, then please leave!" she said in a trembling voice.

"Oh, please don't be frightened! I am merely a traveler looking for a place to rest for a while."

"Where do you come from and where are you going?"

"I come from Memphis! I was just travelling and exploring the area."

"So you're Egyptian!" The girl stopped trembling and relaxed a bit.

"My father died recently so I wanted to get away from Memphis for a while. I needed to cool my head."

"I'm so sorry to hear that! My father died recently too."

"My deepest sympathies! I understand how you must feel," said Qaroon.

"If you wish, you may rest here for a little bit. I have some food to share," said the girl.

"Oh no, I don't want to trouble you!"

"There is no trouble at all! Please!" She motioned him to take a seat under the tree.

Qaroon took a seat and she went to get some food from her sack. She took a seat in front of him and gave him some bread and cheese. They sat down and ate for a while.

"How did your father die, if you don't mind me asking?" Qaroon asked.

The girl looked at the ground and teared up.

"I am so sorry! I didn't mean to upset you," said Qaroon.

"No, it's fine!" She looked at Qaroon. "He was killed by Israelites."

"That is horrible!"

"Those animals will not get away with what they did!" the girl said in an angry voice.

"Can you really blame them?" asked Qaroon.

"Excuse me? So they had a right to kill my father?" The girl seemed mad.

"I mean, they have been enslaved and humiliated for centuries. Egyptians slaughtered them, raped their women and daughters, and killed their children. Something like this was bound to happen."

"Those animals deserve all of that and more! Why are you defending them?"

"I'm not defending them. I'm just saying that they are people as well. How would you feel if you were one of them? Would you not crave the taste of revenge?"

"Are you sure you are from Memphis? I hear the people of Memphis despise Israelites above all else."

"May I ask why you despise them?"

"Because they are traitors who supported the Hyksos!"

"Their ancestors supported the Hyksos! Why does a son have to suffer the sins of his father?"

"That's just how things are!" the girl said dismissively.

"Really?" Qaroon gave her a doubtful look. "And why is that?"

"You have to punish the son for the sins of his father so that he may never repeat them again. It must forever be remembered!"

"Imagine yourself in their situation. Does that really seem fair?" Qaroon asked.

"I don't care what's fair! What I care about is those filthy animals getting what they deserve!"

"Haven't they suffered enough already?"

"What kind of Egyptian defends those worthless slaves?" The girl gave him a judgemental look. "They haven't suffered enough! They need to learn their place!"

"Just imagine you were an Israelite. Any Egyptian man has the right to rape you and suffer no consequence."

She did not reply.

"Here's what I will say to you! You feel the need to avenge your father. Well, they feel the need to avenge the tens of thousands of fathers, sons, wives, daughters, and other relatives that have been raped or killed."

"They would have done something about it already! They will not because they are accepting their place under our feet! They are accepting their place as our property! As our slaves!" the girl said in pride.

Before Qaroon could reply, the girl got up.

"I have to get back to work. So if you don't mind..."

Qaroon got up. "Of course! Thank you so much for your hospitality. But before I go, may I know the name of my generous host?"

"It's Iras, daughter of Kawab."

"Pleasure to meet you, Iras. I am Qaroon, son of Izhar, of Goshen!" He smiled.

The girl was shocked and took a step back. "You're..."

"Yes, I am! I am an Israelite..."

She started walking back slowly and Qaroon started walking towards her at the same pace.

"I am the filthy animal who hasn't suffered enough."

She continued walking backwards, with Qaroon matching her pace.

"I am the son that is suffering for his father's sins, the one who must continue to suffer at the hands of the Egyptians so that I may never forget my ancestors' mistakes."

She continued walking back in horror. Qaroon walked towards her until her back hit a tree. She was cornered. Qaroon took a couple more steps towards her and then stopped.

"And you, my dear, are the foot that is stepping on my back. You are the whip that has been hurting my people for centuries! You represent the very body of the thousands of Egyptians who have raped thousands of women and killed tens of thousands of Israelites."

Qaroon grabbed her by the shoulders. There was no point resisting. He was too strong.

The girl started to cry. "Please!"

"Please what? Please don't?" Qaroon looked her in the eyes and smiled. "You are about to feel what thousands of women before you have felt. You will know just how helpless and powerless they all were."

"Help!" The girl started to scream but was muffled by Qaroon's hand on her mouth.

"Don't bother screaming! We're the only people out here for a good distance!"

Qaroon pinned her against the tree and started ripping her clothes off.

"One more thing! Please believe me when I say that I am not doing this out of revenge for my people." He threw a piece of her clothing on the ground. "I hate Israelites just as much as you do. Perhaps even more! Those morons are part of the reason why you Egyptians have enslaved us."

Qaroon continued to talk calmly as he ripped her clothes off. She cried and tried to scream but was unable to because of Qaroon's hand, which was now wet with her tears.

"I'm only doing this because of what I have suffered as an Israelite because of people like you, and because you were being very rude and got on my nerves. Just like your father!"

The girl's eyes widened.

"He was being extremely rude, calling me and my friend names and throwing rocks at us, so I killed him," Qaroon said as he finished taking off the last piece of her clothes. "Did he deserve to die? Perhaps. Do you deserve to suffer for his sins? Definitely! Why? Because this is how things are." He turned her around and grabbed both of her hands with one arm, while the other hand was over her mouth. "I have no idea what this will feel like for you, but I imagine it's going to hurt."

Later, Qaroon started walking back to Goshen. Before he entered the cornfield, he looked behind him at the naked corpse of the girl on the ground under the tree.

In the early morning, under the old sycamore tree, Izhar was eating old cheese with dry bread. Qaroon was gathering the sheep around the tree. He came back to his father, sat down, and started eating.

"Father?" asked Qaroon. "Do you remember what we talked about when we were coming back from Heliopolis? About you selling half of your sheep?"

"What took you so long? I thought you were just tired that night so you were speaking nonsense," Izhar said, chewing on a piece of bread. He then swallowed the bread and turned to face Qaroon. "Tell me, son, I want to know what's on your mind."

"Tell me this first. Do you trust me?"

"As a son, of course, but as a tradesman or experienced merchant, definitely not! I will admit that I am curious about what you're planning." Izhar paused for a moment. "I am willing to risk losing half my sheep for the sake of becoming the richest man in Israel," he said in a mocking tone. "Only if your plan actually makes sense. Now, tell me! What is your plan?"

"I remember when Father Lawi talked about Joseph and his time in Egypt. Also, he mentioned the history of our people since they came to Egypt in the days of the Hyksos. Those were the only useful things that ever came out of Father Lawi's mouth. When I heard his tales, I decided that I want to be like him."

"Who? Father Lawi?"

"Father Lawi?" Qaroon asked in a disgusted tone. "I mean Joseph."

Izhar gave Qaroon a confused look. "You mean you want to be a prophet?"

"Of course not! Imagine me as a prophet… Ha! The idea alone makes me laugh. I mean to be as rich as Joseph was. He was an Israelite, but somehow, he made himself into a wealthy Egyptian."

"You want to be rich?" Izhar laughed. "Not only that, but you also want to be Egyptian? Grow up, Qaroon! We're slaves! At any time, the Egyptians can walk over here with their swords and whips and force us to build them a pyramid." Izhar took a bite out of his bread. "How exactly do you plan to become a rich Egyptian? The only reason Joseph succeeded was because he was a prophet and God was on his side. He was also sold to one of the king's officials of Egypt at the time. Do you plan on being sold to the Pharaoh?"

"Don't mock me, old man!" said Qaroon in a joking tone. "Just because you have no ambitions or dreams doesn't mean that you can run around crushing those of other people. Not all of us want to herd sheep until we die,"

"I'm not mocking you. Well, I am, but it's because what you're trying to do is impossible."

"When Joseph was released from prison, didn't the king appoint him over the treasures of Egypt?"

"That was only because he interpreted the king's dream of the seven fat cows being eaten by the starving ones, and the dream actually came true after a few years. Joseph saved Egypt. That's the only reason the king appointed him as treasurer."

"Yes, it was that dream that made Joseph rule Egypt, and the same dream will lead me even higher!"

"You want to walk up to the front gates of the palace and tell them that you're a prophet that can interpret dreams? 'Let me in please, Pharaoh, and make me your treasurer!'" Izhar laughed.

"I am serious, Father! Enough mocking me!"

"I'm only joking, Qaroon! Lighten up! Now, please tell me what is it you want me to do with my sheep. I'm curious to see how long it will take you to give up on this plan of yours."

"I will do what Joseph did. The Nile flood comes in cycles, some years high and others low. When the Nile flood goes down and the Nile runs dry, farmers store their harvest. Now, imagine someone acquires all of their harvest. All of it! Every harvest in all of Egypt, owned by one man."

"You?"

"I will be the only one in Egypt to have what everyone needs! Everyone in Egypt will come to me begging. I will store all of the grains in granaries."

"But how are you going to build these granaries? The amulet that you found is definitely not enough. You need a hundred more to build them. Granaries are not cheap!"

"I'll think about that later. But what do you think?"

"A good idea, although I doubt you'll be able to make any of it happen. But let's say you succeed: are you going to sell grains to Israelites? They are poor."

"Of course, Father. But only if they can afford it. Nothing in this world is free! But forget about them. Are you going to sell half of your sheep or not?"

"Forget it. I won't even sell one sheep for this mad plan of yours."

"You don't want to be the richest man in Israel?"

"Your visit to Heliopolis has driven you out of your mind!" Izhar laughed, and Qaroon shook his head.

CHAPTER 3

"FROM AN ISRAELITE TO AN EGYPTIAN."

A few years later, Qaroon had grown into a muscular and handsome young man. He was walking alone in the Heliopolis marketplace wearing an Egyptian smock with a leather belt around his waist. He wore a deer skin around his left shoulder and a black coral necklace. The marketplace was as crowded as usual. Qaroon went in a stroll around the market. It was exactly the same as the first time he saw it with his father—the yelling merchants, the endless merchandise being bought and sold, and the long lines of slaves being offered. After his walk in the market, he headed to Helal's hut on the Nile bank. When he arrived, he saw Helal sitting in the shadow of a big tree, eating with two young men.

"Good morning, good men," Qaroon said.

They looked at him in confusion.

"Who are you?" Helal asked.

"It's me, Adham! My father and I stayed the night in your hut a few years ago and you offered us food."

Helal was silent for a few moments. "Adham? The son of Badri! Welcome, my son. Come and sit down. Join us please. How is your father?"

"He is good. He sends his greetings to you."

"Where is he? Isn't he with you?" asked Helal.

"No, I came by myself this time," Qaroon replied. He looked at the two young men who were gazing at him.

"These are my sons, Minali and Daniali."

They greeted Qaroon and smiled. Qaroon started to eat with them. After they finished, Qaroon and Minali went to have a walk around the field. Helal and Daniali walked down the field checking and inspecting bean and onion scrubs. The four men met at the other side of the field.

"Let's go now, Adham," Helal said.

"Where to, father Helal?'

"Home. Or will you spend the night in the hut?" asked Helal.

"I'd be asking too much of you. I'm afraid to be a burden," said Qaroon.

"Don't say that, son. It would be a pleasure to have you as our guest," said Helal.

They walked along the dirt road heading to Helal's home.

Helal's house was built of mud and straw bricks. It was located at the end of the dirt road that passed by his field. It was a simple one story house surrounded by a small garden. In the garden, there were several palm, guava, and pomegranate trees. The path leading to the door was covered with a big grape bush. A cask of water was placed at the door beside a clay platform. Helal knocked on the door. A few moments later, a girl opened it. They entered and Qaroon kept gazing at the girl. She blushed when she saw him with her father.

"Don't be shy, Lamia. This is my young friend, Adham. Are still carving your palm leaf plate?"

"Yes, Father. I will finish it by tomorrow," she replied in a shy tone. She walked away.

"After we have something to eat, you can go to sleep in Minali and Daniali's room."

"Are we going to sleep this early?"

"We have to be in the field tomorrow at dawn."

A few days later, Qaroon was sitting with Minali in front of the hut. They had a fire lit and were roasting some corn cobs and drinking grape wine.

"So you work with your father, Minali, right?" Asked Qaroon.

"Yes, but I just can't stand it. I wish I could wake up one morning and just be so rich that I wouldn't have to work ever again."

"How do you expect to be rich without at least a bit of work to get there?"

"I don't know. What do you do for living, Adham?"

"I'm a shepherd like my father. We herd sheep most of the time. My dream is just like yours, only I'm willing to put in a bit of effort to achieve my dream."

"Sheep herding can make you rich?" Minali laughed.

"Of course not, but I know a way to make us both rich—so rich that our slaves will have slaves of their own."

"That wine is really messing with your head, Adham." Minali laughed again. "How exactly do you plan to be that rich?"

"You have to promise me that this will be our secret. No one can know what I am about to tell you," said Qaroon.

"So, you're not drunk? You're actually serious about this?" Minali asked.

"I'm not drunk. Will you listen?"

"I will! Go on!" said Minali.

"Do you promise that not a word of what I will tell you will leave the two of us?"

"I promise you."

"First tell me, where do you bury the dead in Heliopolis?"

"On the west bank of the Nile. Why do you ask?"

"And you put gold, jewelry, and gems in their graves and tombs?" asked Qaroon.

"This is done with the mummies of Pharaohs and kings, not with ordinary people. If we have gold, we wouldn't bother putting it with the dead," replied Minali.

"What do you think the dead do with all that treasure? Wouldn't it be better if they give this gold to the poor?"

"I hope you're not suggesting we raid the tombs of Pharaohs, Adham. Pharaohs are Gods. Robbing the tomb of a Pharaoh is an unGodly crime. We will surely be punished for it in the afterlife. Not to mention tortured and killed in this life as well."

"Do you actually think that they will come back from the dead to spend such fortunes? I do not believe these lies. The living are more worthy of these fortunes. We need it more than they do."

"So you want to break into a tomb and steal the gold of the dead? The tomb of a Pharaoh?" asked Minali fearfully.

"Yes! But this isn't exactly stealing. We need it more than they do. It is our right. We have to take what's ours since it won't be given to us," Qaroon said with an angry tone.

"But this gold is cursed. The temple priests have cursed the gold with black magic and witchcraft. You will burn the moment you touch it. It is said that if anybody approaches the tombs, he will be turned into a monkey. And if he somehow manages to go through the doors, he will be transformed into a pig."

"Monkeys and pigs? That is all nonsense. They just make up these rumors so people like you don't go near the tombs. I've been to the pyramids. I didn't grow fur or start eating shit, now did I?" Qaroon laughed.

Minali didn't speak for a while, and no sounds were heard except for them chewing and drinking wine.

"But Adham, do you think it's easy to break into a tomb? If it was, I'd imagine a lot of people would have tried by now."

"That's true, but I think most people just don't want to risk becoming pigs," said Qaroon. "This is our advantage. We'll be the rare few who actually try to raid a tomb."

"I hope you're right. Otherwise, we'll risk breaking in and then finding the tomb already raided—or worse, we'll actually become pigs."

"We won't go for the big pyramids. We'll go for some of the less guarded tombs in Memphis."

"Memphis?" asked Minali.

"Yes, I know that many Pharaohs are buried there. There is a big pyramid there. It's not as big as the ones here, but still big enough to have enough gold to make us both rich for life. People call it Sakkara's pyramid."

"How are we going to break through a pyramid?"

"We don't have to. We have nothing to do with the pyramid. We are going to search in the tombs around it, in the guarded area."

"I am so afraid, Adham."

"Afraid of being rich?"

"Afraid of getting caught or getting turned into a pig."

"Not so much afraid to be a monkey?"

"At least I'll have thumbs to hold stuff. But if I'm a pig, I'll have to eat shit."

"Don't be afraid. We are going to be the wealthiest people in Egypt. Believe me."

"What are we going to do about the guards?" asked Minali in a worried tone.

"I'll tell you later. By the way, I'm leaving today. We'll meet tomorrow in Amun's temple at sunrise."

"What am I going to tell my father?"

"Tell him anything, like you are going to the market to buy some meat. Remember, no one knows what we are up to."

"It's a deal. How are we going to Memphis?"

"You'll know everything in time. Let's go back inside now. I want to say goodbye to your family."

They put the fire out and went back in the house.

At dawn the next day, Qaroon stood beside one of the pillars of Amun's temple. He had his tools and equipment on the backs of two donkeys. Before sunrise, he saw Minali running in a hurry.

"It was hard to convince my father. He's very suspicious," said Minali while panting.

"Does he know you're coming to meet me?" asked Qaroon in a worried tone.

"No, but he kept asking me where I'm going. He wanted to send Daniali with me, but I insisted on going alone." He turned and looked at the donkeys in surprise. "Are those your donkeys?"

"Our donkeys. We are partners now, Minali. Let's go!"

They got on the donkeys and headed south. The dirt road was empty except for some farmers who were going to their fields with cows, donkeys, and camels. When they were halfway between Heliopolis and Memphis, they stopped to rest in the shadow of a big berry tree.

"Minali, go to that field over there and bring us some radishes and some beans to eat," said Qaroon.

Minali went over to the field and disappeared for some time. When he returned, he had some green beans and radish leaves for him and Qaroon. He also brought corn sticks for the donkeys. They were starving, so they sat to eat. Minali kept looking at the golden wheat fields around them.

"Hatur is the month of golden fields."

"In a few days you will be the owner of a golden fortune."

"Do you actually think we'll find something?"

"Sure. The whole west bank is full of pharaonic tombs and graves. Mummies and rotten dead bodies don't deserve the treasures buried with them. They don't need it."

"You don't believe in another life after death?"

"Is there any proof of such myths? They're just lies that were invented and are now held as facts. Even if they were true, sooner or later someone is going to rob these graves. I'm sure of it. Why wait until it's all stolen when we can take some now?"

"You are right! I don't think these myths are true. I think the temple priests invented all this to keep their fortunes. When should we arrive at Memphis?"

"At this pace, we'll be there before sunset."

"What are these robes for?" asked Minali.

"You'll know everything in time."

"How are you going to handle the guards?"

"They will like what I have for them."

"What's that?"

"Opium."

"Opium? Give me some!"

"No, not now. I don't want you doped. I need you fully alert. I'll give you a lot of opium to celebrate when we are done with our mission. Let's pick up the pace; we want to be there before sunset."

After several hours, they arrived at the Sakkara pyramid.

"That is the pyramid I told you about. See how different it is?" asked Qaroon.

"What are we going to do now?"

"We'll find a place to spend the night. Tomorrow we cross the Nile to the west side."

As the sun was rising the next day, Qaroon and Minali were on a wooden boat. The boatman was rowing towards the west side of the Nile. They didn't talk until the boat hit the sandy beach. Qaroon thanked the boatman and gave him a piece of silver. The boatman was pleased and looked at the silver with a greedy smile. He pushed the boat away from the sand and rowed back to the east side. They both watched him row away and then started walking towards the pyramid. Their feet sank in the soft sand as they got closer. They sat to rest on a wide stone platform, which seemed to be a sign indicating the burial site.

"It's not going to be easy. This is a very large area. Where do we even start?" Minali asked desperately.

"Don't worry. First, we should find a place to hide our tools. After that, we make a tour around the pyramid to see what we are going to do."

"I want to sleep for a bit. I am too tired to go on."

"You can sleep here while I go walk around," said Qaroon

"Don't go too far."

Minali lay down on the ground, put his sandals under his head, and fell asleep. Qaroon started walking around the area. Suddenly, he heard a harsh voice behind him. He turned to find an over-sized guard carrying a large axe over his shoulder.

"Who are you?" yelled the guard.

"Good sir, you scared me!"

"Tell me who you are! What in the name of Ra are you doing here?"

"I'm Adham of Memphis. I'm here to pay tribute to the dead."

"Pay them, or rob them?" asked the guard in a hostile tone.

"I beg your pardon, good sir, but I am not a thief. What is your name?"

"Why do you want to know my name?" The guard started to walk closer in an intimidating way. He could easily cut off Qaroon's head with that axe.

"To get to know each other so we can become friends. I have some grape wine. Interested?" asked Qaroon. He tried not to look terrified of the man that was about to kill him.

"Wine? You have wine here?" The guard loosened up.

"I have food too, friend. So what is your name?"

"Battari. My name is Battari. Where is this wine?" He was starting to lose his temper.

"At the platform with my friend Minali. Let's go there."

They walked together to the platform. Qaroon looked so small compared to Battari. No wonder they hired him as a guard.

"Tell me why you are here," said Battari.

"I told you, to pay tribute to the dead."

"No one comes here to pay tribute the dead. Tell me the truth," Battari said. He placed the axe over his shoulder as if threatening to swing it.

"The truth is that my friend, Minali, had a big fight with his father, so I brought him here for two or three days until things cool off."

"Oh, I see. You came here to clear your minds. And that's why you have wine!"

"And opium," said Qaroon.

"Opium?" Battari's eyes widened and he smiled.

When they arrived at the platform, Minali was still asleep.

"Minali! Wake up! Wake up and meet my friend, Battari."

Minali woke up suddenly, rubbed his eyes, and looked at them while they sat on the floor beside him. He was horrified by the sight of Battari and the axe on his shoulder.

"It's good to meet you, Battari," said Minali in a trembling voice. "I like your axe."

"How very kind of you. I sharpened it this morning in case I needed to cut any heads off. You can never be too sure." Battari laughed.

Minali was terrified by the man's morbid laugh but tried to smile.

"And where do you stay, Battari?" asked Qaroon.

"In a room by the south burial site. I go back to my family in Memphis once every week."

"And you are here all alone? I mean, does anyone replace you when you leave to your family?" asked Qaroon.

"Of course, my friend Sondosi replaces me. He just left for Memphis yesterday," said Battari.

Qaroon got a bottle of wine out of his bag. He filled a cup for Battari, who drank it in one shot. An hour passed as they talked and Battari drank. After several cups, he became so drunk that his speech slurred. Minali tried to drink a lot as well but Qaroon stopped him.

"Can we be your guests for the next two days, Battari?" asked Qaroon.

"Of course, you are most welcome," said Battari. He hiccupped.

"Thank you, Battari, my friend. Thank you," said Qaroon while he filled another cup of wine for him. They kept talking and laughing. Qaroon hid hatchets and the other tools in the mat. Minali carried the mat on his shoulder. Qaroon carried a big bag on his back and they followed Battari to his room.

When they arrived at Battari's room, he pointed with his axe to two nearby hills.

"That is the southern burial site," said Battari.

The room had no door. It was built of large bricks with a low ceiling. At the entrance, he put a water cask with a wooden cover. On the floor, there was an old cow skin carpet. His bed was built of bricks in the corner and covered with a sheep's fur and a straw pillow. On the wall was an oil lantern.

Battari and Minali stepped inside the room while Qaroon sneaked to the back, where he hid the mat with the tools. He placed it behind a big rock and went back to them.

"This is my room! What do you think?" said Battari. For some reason, he was extremely proud of his room.

"A very good room, my friend. We are afraid that we're bothering you or invading your privacy."

"Not at all. On the contrary, you are going to entertain me. I'm bored out of my mind here and I only have corpses for company."

"Does anybody come here at all?' Qaroon asked.

"Rarely! Most of the time it's when they're burying the dead. But sometimes, tomb raiders come here and try to steal the buried treasures. Not on my watch," Battari said. He swung his axe across the room a couple of times. "Ha!"

Minali gave Battari the same look of terror as before. He then gave Qaroon a worried look.

"You mean burying the Pharaohs?" asked Qaroon.

"A Pharaoh or an ordinary Egyptian."

"Are they buried in the same place?"

"No, the tombs of the Pharaohs are on the southern hill, while the people's graves are in the northern areas. You said you have opium?"

"You deserve the best, my friend," Qaroon said with a smile. He kneeled to open his bag and took out a piece of cloth, where he had carefully wrapped a big piece of brown opium. He cut a small piece with his teeth and handed it to Battari.

"How should it be taken? It's the first time for me to try it," said Battari.

"I thought you were an opium expert because of the way you smile when I mention it." Qaroon smiled.

"Not really, but my replacement guard, Sondosi, told me it does wonders. I've been waiting impatiently to try it out. Now, tell me, how do I do this?"

"Cut a small piece, put it under your teeth, and suck on it. You will feel like a Pharaoh!"

"I'm so tired," said Minali, yawning. "I'm going to sleep." A few moments later, they heard him snoring. Battari bit a piece of opium and showed it to Qaroon, who smiled at him and nodded. He placed it under his teeth and closed his mouth. He kept looking at Qaroon. Battari's sight started to become hazy and blurred.

"Tell me, my friend, do thieves really come here to rob the tombs?"

"They do not give up. They always come. It's the only thing that makes my job fun. What makes my job easier is that they rarely ever find the entrance to the tombs. Even if they found it, they still wouldn't be able to find the main burial room," Battari said in slurred words.

"The room with the gold inside?"

"Yes!"

"Can you show me one of these tombs? I wish to see it from the inside."

"Of course! There is one open tomb beneath the southern hill.

"Was it robbed?'

"No, the thieves didn't have enough time to find the main burial room. I caught them before they found it and cut their arms off." Battari gave a drunken smile. "I love this axe."

"When was that?" Qaroon asked.

"On the first day of Hat... Hatu... Hatur, the month of the golden... golden fields." Battari was barely able to speak.

"When are you going to take me there, Battari?"

"Yesterday, I will take you." Battari laughed. "No, no... Tomorrow! Not yesterday. You know why? Because yesterday is... is gone... That's why! Today is... tomorrow's yesterday."

"Sleep now, Battari! We'll talk tomorrow." Qaroon laughed. "Feel like a Pharaoh yet?"

"I am... a God!" Battari threw his axe on the floor and lay on his bed. He crossed his legs and laughed for a few moments.

"I'll take you yesterd..." He fell asleep before completing the sentence.

Battari's loud snoring made Qaroon smile. He stood up, carried his bag, and left the two of them sleeping. He went around the room where he hid his tools and picked up the iron rod. He looked at his shadow to know the time left until sunset. He started walking towards the southern hills.

Only the sounds of the blowing wind and his footsteps on the sand followed him. He kept walking until he reached a passage between two high hills. To the right was the entrance of the first tomb Battari had mentioned. He passed by it and stopped in front the next entrance, which appeared to be recently broken through.

He lowered his head, went through the door, and stood for few moments to adapt to the dark.

He walked down the corridor until it was completely dark. Then, he took out an oil lantern from his bag and lit it. His shadow on the coloured walls looked so terrifying that he was startled. But he kept going down the corridor until he reached an open stone door that led to a wide room. He entered carefully, raising his lantern to see around him. He put his bag on the floor and stepped beside the walls, which were full of coloured Pharaonic drawings and hieroglyphic writings. Even the ceiling was covered. A big black box occupied the left corner of the room. Its marble cover seemed impossible to move. He began to speak to himself.

"This room is just an entry to the tomb. The burial room should be behind these walls."

He got closer to the walls and felt them with his palm. There were no elevations, junctions, or bumps. "There must be a door to that room," he said to himself. He kept searching the walls again and again. He headed to the center of the room and sat on the floor. "If I were him, I would make the door in a place no one could find. What is the last place someone would think of in here?"

He placed the lantern on the marble box and opened his bag. He picked a metal horn as long as his forearm. Its wide end was covered with a thick leather band. He stuck the broad end on the wall and his ear on the narrow end. He held a large pebble in his other hand. He knocked on the wall with the pebble and listened through the horn. He didn't hear anything. He was tired after trying a few of times, so he sat down.

"There is nothing behind these walls. Where are you, damned Pharaoh?" He slammed the floor with his fist but then laughed because he remembered his father's sheep, Pharaoh, that would always run towards the cornfield.

Suddenly, his eyes widened in the dim light of the lantern. He picked up the cone, put it against the floor, and knocked a few times with the pebble. He moved around the room, knocking and listening, until he reached the marble box. When he knocked on the floor near the box, he smiled. "It's down here. This floor stands between me and my riches. Getting through this floor will change me from a slave to a master. From a filthy beggar to the person people beg. From an Israelite to an Egyptian." Qaroon smiled.

He stepped back from the marble sarcophagus and repeated his procedure just to be sure. He collected his tools in the corner, took the lantern, and walked out of the tomb.

When he stepped outside of the tomb, he took a deep breath, looked up to the full moon, and smiled as he walked back to Battari's room. There, he prepared the equipment he and Minali needed for the tomb raid. When he was done, he snuck into Battari's room and found him and Minali still sleeping. He was exhausted so he looked for a place to sleep. He found a mat made of sheep fur on the floor so he lied down on top of it and was asleep in seconds.

Sometime later, Minali woke up. The room was dark except for the moon light that came in from the door. He snuck up to Qaroon and poked him.

"Adham! Adham, wake up! Don't be lazy," whispered Minali.

Qaroon woke up immediately. "Did you wake him up?" Qaroon looked at Battari, who was still asleep. "Good! Let's go out to talk for a while."

They went out of the room and walked away from it.

"What are we going to do now, Adham?"

"Look, my friend, we will go back there and we will wake him up. I will offer him a good meal of salted fish and wine. We are not going to drink wine, just eat the fish. After he eats and gets drunk, I will give him a big piece of opium to knock him out."

"I want to try opium."

"Not now, you idiot. Our lives are about to change and all you can think about is opium?"

"When are you going to give me some?"

Qaroon sighed. "I'll give you a big piece when we get back."

"When?" asked Minali eagerly.

"Soon. But now, we have to keep that giant pig drugged all today."

"How are you going to do that?"

"How do we get a person drugged, Minali?" Qaroon sighed. "We drug him! I told you, after he eats, I'll give him a big piece of opium that will knock him out for a day."

"And when he sleeps?" Minali asked.

"Then we rape him!" Qaroon said in a mocking tone. "Minali, what is with all the idiotic questions? When he sleeps, we do what we came here to do! Let's go back to him now. Dawn is about to break."

When they entered the room, they found Battari snoring in a deep sleep.

"It's like he hasn't slept in a year," said Minali

"Make some noise to wake him up," Qaroon said loudly.

They started to prepare what they had for breakfast and Battari woke up.

"Who is it? What is this?" Battari said in lazy deep voice.

"Good morning, Battari, my friend. You have been sleeping like a salted fish!"

"Salted… Fish? What is that?"

"We have some delicious breakfast. You must be very hungry."

"Oh yes, I am starving. Feels like I've been sleeping for a week. Is Sondosi here yet?" Battari said while rubbing his eyes.

"You've only been sleeping for a few hours, Battari," said Minali.

Battari looked funny when he yawned. Then he looked up to the salted fish, onions, and lemons. He stood up and rushed outside. It seemed that nature called. Qaroon opened his bag, got out a big piece of opium, and left it on top of his bag so it looked like it was forgotten there. When Battari returned, he saw it and rushed to it rapidly. He hid it in his smock's pocket while Qaroon smiled.

"Did you see? It worked. The pig has taken the bait," Qaroon whispered with a smile.

The three men sat down to eat together. Qaroon always kept Battari's cup filled with wine. When they finished, Battari stretched on the floor laying his hands on his belly.

"Another fish, Battari?"

"No, no, I'm full. Food is going to spill out of my ears!"

Qaroon filled Battari's cup with wine again and Battari sat down and drank it in one shot.

"I shouldn't have done that! My stomach is going to explode," Battari groaned. "When would you (Hiccup) like me to take you to the (Hiccup) Pharaoh's tomb?" He spoke in slurred words.

"Not now, my friend. Let us enjoy the day!"

"You are right. Let me enjoy my time as a Pharaoh," he said just before hiccupping again.

They laughed and talked for a while.

"Go out Minali, collect some firewood for us. We want to cook a goose for lunch," Qaroon said, winking to Minali.

Minali went out and Qaroon pretended to look for something in his bag. Thinking he was unseen, Battari quickly put the whole piece of opium in his mouth. Minutes after, he started to mutter nonsense. His sight began to blur.

"Adham, do you have a twin?" He stood up unsteadily and walked towards the door. He sat on the floor then stretched his legs and arms staring at the clear blue sky. There was a hawk flying high in the sky. Every time he saw a hawk, he counted it.

"There are so many hawks!"

"Yeah, they are too many. Do they always fly up here?" asked Qaroon.

"They come to take the dead to their world."

Minali was watching and laughing. He came closer when Qaroon waved to him.

"Come on, Minali. We have to start moving."

"Where to?"

"Again with the stupid questions? Don't ask. Let's go! We don't want to waste time."

They carried their bags and walked to the rock where Qaroon had hidden hatchets, iron bars, and a big hammer. They carried them together.

"Let's go back to the pig," Qaroon said.

"Why?" asked Minali, surprised.

"To carry him inside the room, just in case someone walks by."

They went back to Battari. They managed to pull his heavy body and drag him inside. He was knocked out. If they didn't know he was drugged, they would've mistaken him for a corpse. They took their stuff and headed to the southern tombs.

After entering the tomb, Qaroon and Minali walked down the long descending corridor.

"Watch your head! The ceiling is low here."

"Have you been here before, Adham?"

"Yesterday, when you were both sleeping."

They walked along the corridor hearing only the echoes of their footsteps and their breathing. When they arrived at the broken wall, Qaroon stopped.

"Move that stone inside," Qaroon said, pointing.

Minali put his things aside and kneeled to push the stone.

"Why?" he asked.

"Do what I tell you! No questions!" Qaroon shouted.

"Why do I have to do all the work? We're partners," complained Minali.

"You didn't even join me yesterday. You just fell asleep," Qaroon said in a stern tone. "So just do what I say for now."

"It's too heavy. Give me a hand," Minali said. He was trying to push the piece of stone but it was barely moving.

Qaroon stepped inside the room and lit the lantern. He went back to Minali and pushed the stone with him. It was truly heavy. They pushed it beside the black marble sarcophagus. They both started panting.

"Grab a hammer! We're going to break through that floor over there," he said, pointing towards the floor at the centre of the room next to the sarcophagus.

"Is the Pharaoh buried down there?"

"Let's hope so."

Qaroon gave the hammer to Minali and he grabbed the hatchet. They started striking the floor in one spot.

After some time, both of them were sweating. The heat in the room was unbearable. It was made worse by the smell of corpses. Qaroon kneeled down on the floor and brought the lamp closer.

"Look! The floor cracked. The smell of corpses is getting stronger so the burial room is definitely down here. Faster, Minali! Faster! We don't want to risk that Nile hippo waking up. Dig like your life depends on it, because it does."

They both struck the floor more violently and eagerly.

Another while later, they had an opening the size of an eggplant.

"I'm so tired," Minali said while panting. "I need food, Adham!"

"But we're so close!"

"I know, but after we're done with the digging, we still have to carry all the gold from down there up here. Then we have to carry it all outside. We need rest!"

"Fine! But no more rest after this. Get us some food," said Qaroon.

They sat on the floor and Minali got old cheese, bread, and a cucumber out of his bag. They ate and drank water without a word. Minali stretched on his back.

"Get up!" Qaroon shouted at him. "Let's get back to work. After we're done here, you can sleep for the rest of your life."

They continued striking and digging again. Eventually, the hole became wide enough for a man to pass through. They stopped digging.

"How are you not tired, Adham?" complained Minali.

"Who said I'm not? I'm more exhausted than you, but at least I'm willing to sacrifice my rest now so I can rest later. All you want to do is rest now," said Qaroon. "Yes, I am very inclined to sleep for a day right now, but I am more inclined to get the gold. Bring me the ropes!"

Minali passed him a set of long ropes. He held a rope in his hand, made a knot around a pebble, and threw it inside the hole. He smiled when he heard it striking the floor seconds later. He pulled it up and measured its length. He then started tying the ropes together, making a ladder. He then threw the rope ladder through the hole and took the other end and tied it firmly to the broken stones at the entrance. The smell was even worse now, like it was trapped for centuries and only now escaping.

"Let's go down, my friend. I'll go first, then you hand me the lantern. When I'm down there, follow me," said Qaroon.

"Will do," said Minali with a neutral expression.

"Minali! You're about to be one of the richest people in Egypt. Why are you not excited?" Qaroon asked.

"I'm just tired," Minali said, yawning.

Qaroon shook his head and inserted his legs in the opening of the hole. It was pitch black inside. He started slowly climbing down the rope ladder. When he disappeared in the hole, Minali could barely see him. Minali then saw Qaroon extending his hand and Minali handed him the lantern. A minute later, the ladder stopped shaking.

"You can come down now! Just make sure the rope is secure so we don't get stuck down here."

Minali checked the rope and then started making his way down. When Minali's feet hit the ground, he looked around to find Qaroon shining the lantern around the room. There was a big white marble sarcophagus in the middle. The walls were all covered with pharaonic drawings and hieroglyphic writings. Many marble, stone, and clay jars were arranged beside the walls.

Several stone statues of a Pharaoh were placed around the sarcophagus. In one corner was a gold coated chair and a large bed. In the opposite corner, six closed wooden boxes were placed together. The third and the fourth corners were occupied by long shelves on which stone and wooden statues of pharaonic Gods were placed, all facing the sarcophagus.

"Do you see what I see?" Qaroon asked with wide eyes.

"I can't believe my eyes. Adham. You are a genius!"

"Pass me the iron bar!" Qaroon said.

"It's up there."

"Then go up there get it!" Qaroon said angrily. "Get the hammer too!"

Minali obeyed at once and went up. Moments later, he called Qaroon.

"Adham, get away from the ladder, I'm going to throw them."

He threw the bar and the hammer. Qaroon took the bar and forced open the first wooden box. Minali climbed down the rope ladder. The box was full of golden statues, icons, amulets, beetles, and crowns. All glimmered in the dim light of the lantern. They both looked astounded by the bright flickering of gold.

"Let's open the second box, lift it with me," said Qaroon.

They opened the rest of the boxes. Five of them were filled with golden and silver statues and artifacts. When they opened the sixth box, the found a large golden mask studded with gems.

"What we'll do first is separate gold from silver. This won't take time. Come on, Minali, let's do it."

They kneeled on the floor, grabbing and separating pieces into two big piles. The golden pile was bigger. Qaroon took the mask, turned it face down, and filled it with gold. They both filled their bags with gold. They became noticeably heavier.

"When I go up, I'll throw you a rope to tie it to the mask. After I lift it up, we'll do the same with the two bags. Then you can climb up and we can go live like kings."

Qaroon climbed the rope ladder. When he was up, he threw the rope to Minali, who did as Qaroon told him. They repeated this four times until all the gold was up with Qaroon.

"Is there any gold left?" asked Qaroon.

"No, the rest is all silv..."

Before Minali could finish his sentence, Qaroon quickly pulled the rope ladder up, stranding Minali in the burial room.

"You can keep the silver, I don't need it," Qaroon said with a sinister smile.

"Very funny, Adham," Minali said, letting out a fake laugh. He then looked at Qaroon's face and saw how serious he was.

"Adham? You're not actually going to leave me here, right?" Minali said in a terrified voice.

"Listen to me, you filthy Egyptian. My name is not Adham. I'm Qaroon from Israel. Those who you Egyptians have enslaved for centuries," he yelled.

"Please don't do this! You can keep the gold. All of it! Just please don't leave me here," Minali said. He started to cry.

"You believe in the afterlife, right? So you can go to your Gods and tell them what Qaroon did to you."

"Qaroon or Adham, whatever your name is, please! I swear I'll forget this ever happened. I'll let you have all the gold and I won't tell a soul," said Minali. He got down on his knees and started begging.

"By the way, didn't you want to try opium? Here is a big piece just for you. If you take in your mouth, you'll feel like a Pharaoh." Qaroon burst into sinister laughter and threw a piece of opium to Minali, who started to scream and cry. "Just don't forget to share it with our dead friend in the coffin. After all, you will both be spending eternity together." Qaroon continued his laughter.

"Please, Adham, don't leave me!"

"It's nothing personal, Minali. I can't have you telling anyone about what happened here. As long as you live, you're a liability,"

Qaroon said as he moved back and started pushing the large stone towards the hole. "Second, this is my way of proving to myself that you Egyptians are not truly superior to me. Burying you alive just shows me how insignificant you really are." Qaroon continued to slowly push the large stone towards the hole.

Minali was screaming his lungs out, calling for his father and brother, his mother and his sister. He called for many Gods to save him. He even called for Battari.

"Not even a God can save you, Minali. In here, at this very moment, I am God! I have your life in the palm of my hands. I control whether you live or die," Qaroon shouted.

"Qaroon!" Minali shouted.

Minali's screams echoed through the tomb but they slowly got lower and lower, not because Minali wasn't trying hard enough, but because the hole to his freedom was slowly being covered up. His voice was slowly being muted. He knew screaming could not save his life, but what else could he do? Minali hopelessly screamed and cried while Qaroon continued to push the big stone towards the hole. After that... Silence! Qaroon smiled as he heard the final echoes of Minali's screams fade away.

When Qaroon came out of the tomb, the light of the sun blinded his eyes. He carried an iron bar on his shoulder with one bag hung each side of it. In his hands, he carried the other tools and the ropes. He walked slowly until he entered the corridor of the first tomb. He threw the ropes on the ground, lit the lantern, and threw it on the ropes, setting them on fire. He put the hammer in one of the bags. When the ropes were turned to ash, he carried his bags and went back to Battari's.

When he arrived at the room, he hid his bags behind the rock. He smiled when he saw Battari sleeping. His snoring was as loud as ever. He picked up the wine bottle and shook it.

"There still is one more cup for you, Battari." He poured what was in the bottle in a cup. He took out a small bottle from his pocket which contained a brown powder. He emptied the powder into the wine.

"Sorry, Battari, my friend, but you have to die, because you are also a liability," he said it out loud as he was certain Battari could not hear him.

"Battari! Battari! Wake up, my friend!" Qaroon said as he shook the man.

Battari moved like a buffalo and started kicking. He then raised his head and looked at Qaroon. He sat down on the bed and saw the cup of wine. He took it in his hand and drank it all at once. His sight was still hazy and blurred.

"We have to go now, Battari. Thank you so much for letting us stay here," said Qaroon.

"Where to?" said Battari, his voice slurred.

"Home. We'll leave you to rest. Sleep well, Battari, my friend. Goodbye."

Battari tried to stand up but he couldn't. He just fell on the bed. Qaroon went to the back to get his bags and headed towards the Nile.

Qaroon arrived at the Nile bank at midnight. He walked in the bushes and chose a hidden place between two high rocks, put down his load, and laid down on the ground. He was so exhausted that he fell asleep the moment he laid his head on one of his bags.

Qaroon woke up some time later the voice of an angry man. He looked through the bushes and saw a man shouting at and cursing crocodiles. It seemed that a crocodile had torn his fishing net apart.

"Damn crocodiles! Damn the Nile! Damn this life!" shouted the man angrily as he threw a rock at a crocodile that was swimming away.

Qaroon emerged from the bushes and waved his hand to the boatman, who was surprised to see Qaroon and rowed towards him.

"What are you doing here?" shouted the man.

"I was visiting my uncle Battari," said Qaroon.

"Battari? He never mentioned having any nephews."

"Can you take me to the other side?"

"How much will you pay me?"

"A piece of silver."

"Two pieces!" the man said greedily.

"Done! I'll get my things."

Qaroon stepped on to the boat with his iron bar and the two bags. He put them on the boat's floor and laid back on the side of the boat. The boatman started rowing while keeping his eyes fixed on the bags, trying to see what was inside them. The man looked at Qaroon and thought that he was asleep. He stopped rowing and kneeled to open one of the bags. As soon as he opened it, a golden statue fell out on the boat's floor. The boatman picked it up and then turned to look at Qaroon. Before their eyes met, he was struck in his face. The statue fell on the boat's floor and so did the boatman. He looked at Qaroon and saw him holding the boat's oar, ready to swing it again. The boatman's head started to bleed.

"You did this to yourself," Qaroon said, shaking his head.

"Did you kill Battari too?" said the boatman, giving him a hostile look.

"Battari was necessary, but you could've minded your own business."

"Curse you!" shouted the man. "Curse you and all men like you. Sobek will not leave this unpunished!"

"Isn't Sobek the crocodile God? Maybe if I offer him a sacrifice, he'll forgive me." Qaroon smiled.

"Tomb raider!" the man shouted.

Qaroon struck him on the head with the edge of the oar. The oar cracked and let out a loud noise—or maybe it was the boatman's skull. Blood started pulsing from the boatman's head. His body trembled as he fell to the side of the boat and died. Qaroon grabbed the stone chair that was on the boat and tied the boatman's body to it. He looked around and saw nobody, so he pushed the stone overboard. Seconds later, the man's body followed. Bubbles were rising to the surface. It wasn't long until the nearby crocodiles started swimming towards the man's corpse. They all dove underwater and Qaroon started to row away. After he put a bit of distance between him and the crocodiles, he looked behind him. The area was covered in blood and an arm broke the surface of the water.

"I hope Sobek is pleased," Qaroon said as he continued to row towards the eastern bank.

The water stream led the boat fast to the shore north of Memphis. When he reached the shore, Qaroon took his bags and jumped to the land. He pushed the boat back to the water and walked over to some nearby bushes. Qaroon walked between the bushes until he found a suitable place to put his things. No one passed through where he was but even if they did, no one could see him. He took the hammer out and began to strike the golden mask, folding and molding it into a large shapeless piece of gold. He started striking statues and bracelets so they would be disfigured and lose their features. Rings and amulets were now thin pieces of gold. He finished the first bag and began to do the same to the contents of the second. He collected jewels and gems in one bag of cloth. The other was filled with the flattened gold pieces. He covered both bags with rags and tied them to a belt. He then put the belt around his shoulder and smiled when he felt how heavy it was. He searched the area around him to find any missed gold and headed towards the road.

After walking for a bit, he was already tired because the gold was too heavy for a man to carry for too long. In the shadow of a big tree, he saw a farmer sleeping. Not so far from him, a cow and a donkey were tied to a tree. Qaroon walked up to the farmer and shook him.

"Who are you?" shouted the farmer as he woke.

"Just a traveler who is in need of a donkey," Qaroon replied.

"Not for sale! Sorry. This donkey has been with me for twenty years. Our bond can never be broken!"

Qaroon took out a piece of gold from his pocket. "That's understandable. The bond between me and my gold can't be broken either." He smiled.

The farmer's eyes widened. "You know what? I don't like the way he looks at my wife. You can have him!"

Qaroon handed the piece to the farmer and went to pack his bags on the donkey. He then set off on the long road back to Goshen.

A few days later, Izhar sat under the old sycamore tree in Goshen's herd lands. His sheep and goats were scattered in front of him. He looked so sad and aggrieved and was drawing lines with a stick on the ground. He lifted his head to see a man on a donkey getting closer. He stood up the moment he knew it was Qaroon and ran towards him. Qaroon got off the donkey and embraced his father. They sat under the old tree.

"How are you, Father?"

"You are a cruel son. Where have you been for the past month?" asked Izhar.

"Has it been a month? It passed by so fast."

"Where were you?"

"Do you remember what we talked about several times?"

"You mean your dreams of being a prophet?"

"No!" Qaroon rolled his eyes. "Being rich."

"Yes, I remember. Have you given up hope on this mad plan of yours?"

"On the contrary, the plan is working out even better than expected."

"What do you mean?"

"Open this bag, Father!" Said Qaroon.

Izhar pulled the thread that tied the bag and put his hand inside it.

His face froze as his fingers touched the gold. He took one piece out and looked at it.

"Gold! All this is gold?" shouted Izhar. "Is it real?" Izhar was shocked.

"Quiet, old man! Yes, it's all real."

"Where did you get it from?"

"It doesn't matter. What matters is that my plan will work now that I have all this gold." Qaroon smiled.

"I have to know where you got all this!"

"No, you don't have to know. Don't make me regret telling you."

"Did you steal it?" asked Izhar

Qaroon did not answer.

"Did anyone see you?"

"Only the dead saw me."

"Clever fox! This gold will help us a lot around the house. I will buy more sheep and a few cows..."

"Sheep and cows?" Qaroon interrupted. "This is enough gold for all of us to go and live away from this damned place and enough for me to continue my plans. And all you can think about is sheep and cows? Are you mad?"

"Watch your tone, Qaroon. You want to go? Go where? We're not going anywhere. The family stays here."

"Fine! You can stay here all you want and spend the rest of your life herding sheep, but I'm taking mother and my sisters with me."

"You'd leave your own father? What makes you think that your mother and sisters will even want to go with you?"

"Because they've suffered enough. Don't you want to forget all the suffering and misery that we've had to deal with our whole lives?"

"We can't leave, Qaroon! This is our life. This is how it has been for centuries and this is how it will be from now on. You just have to accept that."

"You want me to give up this gold that I almost died for so you can buy a few cows and sheep so I can spend the rest of my life in this disgusting village herding them? You want me to get whipped and burned again and watch my mother and sisters get raped? You are not mad, you are something much worse—you are satisfied with your life as a slave. You have somehow adapted to humiliation and torture and watching your son get whipped and your wife and daughters get raped."

"It is better to submit and live than to rebel and die," Izhar said, looking at the ground.

"So be it. If this is how you want to live, then leave me out of it."

"If you want to leave, then leave! But give me my share of this gold."

"Your share? Of what?"

Izhar reached for the bag and Qaroon rudely pushed his hand away.

"Have you gone mad?" said Qaroon. "You don't get one piece! Not even one piece. This gold is mine."

"Qaroon! What is wrong with you? What about your family?"

Qaroon got up and took the bag with him.

"Look, old man! You don't say a word to anyone about what just happened. Don't even mention my name. Forget that I was ever your son."

"This gold has driven you mad," Izhar said while getting up.

"Am I mad for not wanting to live like you? I would rather die than live another day here."

"Listen, Qaroon! Your family is doing very poorly recently. A sickness has killed many of my sheep and it's hard to provide for the family, especially without having you around. So please, spare a few pieces of gold. It is my right to ask this of you."

"How is it your right to ask anything of me?"

"Because I'm your father. I raised you, fed you, and I gave you shelter your entire life without asking for anything in return. This is the only thing that I will ever ask of you. Please, son!"

"I have lived my life with you in poverty, torture, and misery. You've asked me to help you around the house and help you herd your sheep in return for food and shelter. I would say that my debt is paid in full. I owe you nothing."

"Is this what I get after all I've done for you?"

"I should never have come here. I should've stayed in Memphis." Qaroon shook his head. "You will tell no one of this! As of now, you're a liability and you pose a threat to my plans."

"Are you threatening me, Qaroon?"

"Not at all. But keep in mind that the people who know of what I've done have been killed."

"So are you going to kill me as well?" Izhar asked. He seemed disappointed.

Qaroon didn't respond.

Izhar reached for the bag again, but Qaroon pulled it aside and pushed his father violently in the chest. Izhar fell backwards and hit his head on a rock.

Qaroon was frozen still for a few moments. He wasn't sure what had just happened.

"Father?"

There was no reply.

Qaroon kneeled down next to his father and looked into his eyes. All he could see was the look of both shock and disappointment. A pool of blood started to accumulate under his father's head.

"Father?" Qaroon said as one tear started to slide down his cheek. "It was an accident!"

Qaroon shook his father violently, trying to wake him up. But it was too late.

"I never should have come back here. You stupid old man! Your selfishness and greed got you killed. This was all your fault!" Qaroon's expression became more rigid. His eyes were no longer teary. He looked into his father's eyes with hate.

"You were a slave! Just like the rest of them," Qaroon shouted. "I'm better than you. I'm better than all of you. You all accepted your places in this world as slaves! As dirt!" He paused for a moment and got up. He was still looking at his father's eyes. "I went and did something about it. I refused to be a slave like you. And I did it! This was all your fault. You did this to yourself! It wasn't me… It was you!"

Qaroon grabbed the bag of gold off the ground and started walking away. He got on the donkey and started riding towards the borders of Goshen, towards Memphis. He looked back one more time with a look of disgust. He saw the old sycamore tree, and under it, the corpse of his father drowning in a pool of blood.

CHAPTER 4

"THE REMARKABLE ADHAM OF MEMPHIS!"

Many days later, Qaroon handed a man a bag of gold. He smiled and opened it to look inside.

"You will be very pleased with your new house, my lord!" The man said as he extended his arm to shake Qaroon's hand.

"I hope so, my good man." Qaroon smiled and shook the man's hand.

After the man walked away, Qaroon turned to face his new house. It was made of bricks and consisted of two levels. Qaroon went inside and started to take a tour of his new place. The ground floor was a wide hall with a firehouse at its end. Oil lanterns were on every wall and in every corridor. After Qaroon took a quick tour of his new house, he went into the bedroom and sat on the sleeping platform. He then got up, grabbed a hammer and a chisel, and started carving a hole in the center of his bed. After some time, there was a square hole. He emptied his bags of gold inside it and covered it up. After that, he left his house and headed for the market to buy his first possessions.

Qaroon's house was close to the Memphis market. As soon as he exited his house, the sounds of the yelling merchants nearby became louder.

"This is the most comfortable mattress you will ever sleep on!" shouted one of the merchants. "Once you sleep on it, you'll never want to wake up again!"

"Silver necklaces!" shouted another.

"You sir!" said a merchant, getting in Qaroon's way. "Care to buy this chair?" The man pointed to a fancy looking chair next to him. "It's extremely rare and a prized item for its owner."

Qaroon looked at the chair. "I am on my way buy a slave right now. Once I do, I'll come back so that he may carry it for me."

"Very well, good sir." The merchant smiled and stepped aside.

Qaroon continued walking towards the slave trader's market but was drawn to the cheers of a crowd. He looked to his right and saw a large group of people gathering around a man. Qaroon got closer to see what was going on. In the center of the circle was a man holding a stick which had a rope tied to it. The man was moving the stick and the rope was moving along with it. As the rope moved, the crowd cheered and some even retreated in fear.

"What's going on?" Qaroon asked a man standing next to him.

"Can you not see the cobra?" the man shouted. "This man is amazing."

Qaroon waited until the crowd dispersed when the man stopped moving the stick and he walked up to the man.

"The show will resume later! Leave me alone!" the man shouted rudely.

"Watching a man play with a stick is a show?"

The man looked nervous suddenly. "Leave me alone, I say! Or I shall release my cobra at you."

"You mean that rope tied to the stick?" Qaroon smiled and gave the man a doubtful look.

"This is how I make a living and feed my family. I'm sure you understand."

"How do you do it?"

"I will tell you nothing. I have enough competition as it is already."

"That's fine, but do you have any idea who might be able to help me?" Qaroon smiled and took a small piece of gold out of his pocket.

The man quickly took the piece of gold. "Go to Heka's temple and ask for a priest named Amon. Ask him about the rope. Now go away! You're scaring away the crowd."

Heka's temple was a quiet place. The faint sounds of the priests' prayers echoed across the temple. When Qaroon walked into the temple, he marvelled at how massive it was and at the huge pillars carrying the roof. The sun was still rising in the east and the light beamed across the temple onto the giant statue of Heka. Qaroon looked around and saw a few priests walking around the temple. He walked towards one of them.

"Good day to you, sir."

"Good day," the priest said without turning to face Qaroon. "If you want to make a donation, please leave it with Brother Turo. Otherwise, please leave."

"I'm looking for Amon," said Qaroon.

"Why do you seek Brother Amon?" the priest asked in a neutral tone.

"I'm here about the rope."

The priest stopped what he was doing and turned to face Qaroon. "Another one! Why am I not surprised? There's more of you everyday. I am Amon. What is it that you would like to know?" he asked in a neutral tone.

"How does this rope illusion work?" Qaroon asked.

"Have you any idea who Heka is?"

"The God of wasting time?"

The priest rolled his eyes. "Do you want an answer or not?"

"Yes! Yes! Just please, get to the point."

"Very well. Heka is the God of magic and medicine. We, the priests of Heka, serve our God and we preach about him to the public…"

"This is exactly what I mean by wasting time. This information does not concern me," Qaroon said.

"I will give you what you seek. But, you must first meet two of my conditions."

"Name them!"

"You must first make a generous donation to the temple of Heka. Then, you must swear before Heka that you will keep what you learn confidential and not expose it to the public."

"Very well." Qaroon reached into his pocket and took out a small bag of gold. "We both know this isn't going to the temple." Qaroon smiled as he handed it to the priest. "So, why not make both of our lives easier and skip the second condition?"

The priest looked around him to make sure none of the other priests were looking and put the bag of gold in his robes. "Follow me!" he said. He started to walk away.

Qaroon followed Amon down a long corridor. Amon was a tall and slim priest with a short beard. He was wearing a robe that covered his entire body. His voice seemed to be stripped of all emotion. They kept walking until they reached a locked room, which Amon unlocked. The room was quite small but contained hundreds of papyri and scrolls on many shelves. There was a wooden table in the middle with a few scrolls laid out on it. As soon as Amon walked in, he quickly grabbed one of the scrolls from on the table and hid it in his robes. Qaroon pretended not to see him. Amon then turned to the shelves and grabbed three scrolls.

"Take a seat!" Amon ordered.

Qaroon sat down. "Have you read all of these?" he asked, pointing to the scrolls.

"It gets boring working at a temple, so yes," Amon said. He handed Qaroon the three scrolls.

"Is this it?"

"This is everything we have on illusions and enchantment. I will briefly tell you the contents unless you already know how to read."

"Not hieroglyphics."

Amon unrolled the first papyrus and started to read it to Qaroon. "For a subject to be enchanted, they must be weak minded. Even if aware, a weak minded individual can still be enchanted. To successfully enchant the subject, you must first have a strong connection with your demon."

"Demon?" Qaroon asked, surprised.

"Have no fears! If you saw past the illusion of the cobra then your connection with your demon is just fine."

Amon continued reading and Qaroon listened attentively.

"Weak minded people are really that common?" Qaroon asked.

"Think about it this way: You were probably the only person in the entire market today that saw past the illusion. The people are innocent but they are also idiots. They are kind but they are also foolish. They believe anything they are told without questioning the person telling it to them. All their focus lies on the rope when it should really be on the stick. The stick seems to be invisible to them. They only see the rope moving on its own and are then deceived into believing it's a cobra." Amon picked up another scroll. "Shall I continue?"

"Please," said Qaroon.

Amon unrolled the second papyrus. "Demons are evil spirits. They enjoy spreading deceit, evil, lies, and trickery. Each person has their own demon, who accompanies them their entire life..."

"Summarize it for me!" Qaroon interrupted. "How do people believe a rope is a cobra?"

"That man you saw in the market had a strong connection with his demon. The way it works is, his demon communicates with the demons of the crowd and makes them deceive their hosts."

"When I was a child, I saw a cobra. But today, I saw the rope. Why is that?"

"Something changed," Amon said. "You did something that made your demon proud."

Qaroon was silent for a few moments. "Can I see my demon?"

"No one can see or communicate with their demon. Only the demon can see and communicate with the host. The act of enchanting the person in front of you only works if your demon is willing."

"So is that all a demon can do? Change ropes to cobras?"

"Demons are powerful creatures. Once you enchant someone, their free will is inhibited. You can potentially make them believe or do what you want them to."

"How do I know that my demon is willing to cooperate?" Qaroon asked.

"If he refused to let you see the cobra, you can be sure he's cooperative."

"Can you show me how to do it?"

"Much of my time has already been wasted."

Qaroon took out a bag of gold from his pocket and placed it on the table.

Amon looked at the bag of gold. "I will go call one of the apprentices so that we may practice on him."

Amon stepped out of the room and locked the door behind him. He returned some time later with a younger priest who had his eyes wide open and appeared to be enchanted.

"Who are you?" Amon asked.

"I am your servant and slave, master," replied the younger priest.

"What is your purpose in life?" asked Amon.

"To serve you, master."

Qaroon smiled as he watched the young priest respond.

Amon then punched the younger priest in the stomach and there was no response.

"You can order the subject to do whatever you want. At this moment, right here, he has no free will of his own. I can even tell him to take his own life. But here is one thing to keep in mind: We don't know the reason for this, but loud noises seem to cancel the enchantment."

Amon clapped loudly near the young priest's ear and the man started looking around in confusion.

"Where am I, and why does my stomach hurt so much?" he said as he bent over grabbing his stomach.

"Have you been drinking again, you moron?" shouted Amon. "If I tell brother Turo about this, he will kick you out of the temple permanently."

"Please, brother Amon. It won't happen again!"

Amon looked into his eyes and gave him a sharp look. The young priest's eyes expanded again and his expression became neutral. He was, again, enchanted.

"It's your turn!" Amon said, turning to Qaroon.

Qaroon walked up to the younger priest.

"How is this done?" Qaroon asked.

"You know how they say that the eyes are a gateway to the soul?" Amon asked.

"Yes," Qaroon nodded.

"It's actually true. You have to look into the eyes of your target and give them a sharp and intimidating look. Your intent has to be to enchant them and make them submit to your orders. When they sense fear, your demon will do the rest."

After a few tries, Qaroon was successful.

"I'm impressed. It's never that fast for anyone to learn. Your connection with your demon seems to be stronger than most. This makes me curious about the kinds of things you've done in your life since the time you saw the rope as a cobra," Amon said. He gave Qaroon a doubtful look.

Qaroon did not respond.

"What you've done with your life is of no concern to me. Now, send him away but tell him to forget everything he's experienced today."

"You will forget everything you've seen or heard today. Is that clear?" Qaroon asked.

"Yes, master!" replied the younger priest.

"Now, go back to your quarters!"

"Yes, master!" The young priest walked away.

Amon turned towards the table. "I believe I've done my part. My gold, if you may!"

Qaroon placed his hand on the bag of gold. "Not just yet! You can have the gold once you tell me about that scroll you hid in your robes."

Amon gave Qaroon an expressionless look. "Very well. The contents of this scroll will do you no good." He took the scroll out of his robes. "It is a failed experiment by a deceased priest who tried to convert silver to gold."

"I assume you are trying to complete his work?"

"Without success."

"Give me the recipe for this experiment!"

"Why would I do that?" Amon asked.

"Because I wish to recreate this experiment." Qaroon gave Amon a sharp look.

"It won't work on me!" Amon said in a neutral tone. "Once a connection with a demon has been established, the subject can no longer be enchanted. I will, however, overlook your attempt at deceiving me and give you the recipe if you make one more generous donation towards the temple."

Qaroon took out a second bag of gold and placed it on the table. Amon grabbed a scroll off of the shelf behind him and placed it on the table. He sat down and wrote the procedure and recipe of the experiment. He then rolled up the scroll and handed it to Qaroon.

"My gold," he said. He extended his hand.

Qaroon gave Amon the bags of gold.

"Time you were on your way," Amon said as he got up.

Qaroon got up and followed Amon out of the room. Amon locked the room and they both headed for the main temple entrance. Qaroon stepped outside of the temple.

"Good day to you, master Qaroon!" Amon said as he shut the door behind him.

Qaroon looked surprised, but he did not seem worried. He dismissed what had just happened and started walking back towards the market.

Back at the slave market, the merchants were yelling their lungs out, trying to advertise their stock.

"Need help on your farm? This slave can do the work of two mules," shouted a merchant.

"I have beautiful girls like you've never seen before. They will fulfill all your desires and lusts," said another.

"Bandits are everywhere! You need someone like Sharm to protect you. Bandits flee at the sight of him."

Qaroon looked at the merchant's slave.

"He is at the prime of his age! He will last you a lifetime and will be more loyal than a dog," the merchant said. He turned to Qaroon.

Sharm was indeed a large man, similar to the one he saw in Heliopolis with his father. Qaroon walked up to Sharm, who had a look of fear in his eyes. Qaroon gave him a sharp look. Sharm's eyes expanded and his body relaxed.

"You will serve me from now on!" Qaroon ordered.

"Yes, master!" Sharm responded obediently.

"Once I buy you, you will forever be loyal to me. Understood?"

"Yes, master!"

Qaroon gave Sharm another Sharp look. Sharm seemed confused and dazed.

"I wish to buy this slave," Qaroon told the merchant.

"Excellent choice, my lord," the merchant said with a smile.

Qaroon gave the merchant a piece of gold. The merchant signed a piece of paper and handed it to Qaroon.

"Here you are, my lord. This proves your ownership of Sharm."

The village of Ehnees was about a day's walk from Memphis in the middle of vast green lands. Its houses, like any other village, were built with mud and straw bricks. Cows and buffaloes were driven to the fields by children. Several men gathered at the bridge. Two of them stood aside, one old and the other young.

"Who is coming to Ehnees today, Sehami?" asked the young man.

"I don't know. They say he is a man from Memphis coming for business."

"What kind of business?"

"What other kind of business could there be? Maybe he wants to buy beans or grains. The real question is, since when do the merchants of Memphis buy their grains from Ehnees?" Sehami wondered.

"Look over there! I think that's him."

Sehami looked where his friend pointed and he saw a chariot pulled by two horses coming towards the bridge.

"A horse chariot in Ehnees! Our guest must be extremely wealthy."

"Let's welcome him, Sehami."

People gathered around the stranger's chariot. Sharm, who was driving the chariot, stood up.

"Good day to you, townsfolk," said Sharm.

"Same to you, sir," replied some men.

"Where does your mayor live? The one who my master can trade and bargain with?"

"Over there in that white house," said a man among the crowd, pointing.

Sharm sat back down and whipped the horses. They started to run and the chariot went ahead through the village.

It parked in front of the mayor's house, which was easily iden-tifiable. It was a two story house built with white bricks. The mayor was sitting with other men on the front platform, waiting for the coming guest.

"Good day to you, respected mayor," said Sharm as the chariot stopped.

"Same to you, good sir." The mayor got up and turned to face the chariot. "Welcome, respected one," he continued, addressing the man in the chariot.

Qaroon got out of the chariot and Sharm proceeded to introduce him.

"The remarkable Adham of Memphis!"

"We are honored to greet you, great Adham."

"The honor is mine," said Qaroon.

"I'm Samhari, Mayor of Ehnees. Our village is enlightened with your presence."

Samhari called for one of his slaves, who came with a tray with a bottle of wine and clay cups. Samhari filled a cup and handed it to Qaroon.

"Thank you, but I'm here on business."

"This is date wine! You have to drink it!"

"Only this cup for you," Qaroon said with a smile, and started to drink.

"What is the purpose of this visit, great Adham? What can the humble people of Ehnees do for you today?"

"I know this may come as an unusual request, but I would like to build a granary in your village. It won't cost you a thing. The builders will be the people of your village and, of course, they will be paid for their work." He took a sip from his wine.

"You flatter us with your generosity, great one! May I ask about the reason for this sudden charity?"

"I wish to serve the people of Ehnees because I see potential in their growth. Your village, respected mayor, needs a good financial push to compete with the other neighbouring villages. To help your village, I am willing to buy every grain and crop that you harvest this season, and maybe even next season. Do not worry; you will be paid based on the current market price. Not only will you be promoting the wealth of your village, but you will also be contributing to the growth of Egypt. What do you say?"

"Splendid idea! We agree! Don't we, men?" he asked the men accompanying him.

"We agree, respected mayor," replied the men.

"It's a deal then. Now, you ride with me to show me the village and you can choose the place best to build a granary. Tomorrow, we begin building," said Qaroon

Samhari stood up, not believing he was going to ride a horse chariot. He rode on the chariot with Qaroon while Sharm drove it out into the open fields. They cruised between the lands of Ehnees until the mayor chose a piece of land to the west and close to the Nile.

"Samhari, you are different from all the people of Ehnees."

"How so, great one? In the eyes of the Gods, we are all equal."

"You are the mayor, and I heard so many good things about you. You are wise and noble, so I'll pay you double what I pay the other mayors for their support in building the granary."

"I am your servant, great one."

"But this must be between me and you. No one can know."

"Of course, great one."

"And there is something else."

"Your orders!"

"I will entrust you with the building of the granary!"

"You flatter me, great one. What should I do?" asked the mayor.

"You'll employ the builders and manage supplies until the grain house is finished," Qaroon said, putting two golden pieces in Samhari's hand.

"This is too much, great one," he said, pretending to be shocked.

"Let's go now to the owner of the land. I hope he will be easy to deal with like you."

Two days later, workers and farmers were building Qaroon's granary in Ehnees under the direct supervision of Mayor Samhari. In less than a month, it was finished, with a high fence surrounding it. Inside the fence was a wide mortar land with many huge piles of wheat lutes and wood. A wood and iron mill pulled by a bull turned around endlessly, breaking and threshing wheat ears and spikes, extruding grains out of them. Workers used their forks to remove straw, while others collected the grains for the next steps. Work in the grain house never stopped. Workers were everywhere, carrying, grinding, transferring, packing, sorting, and storing. Samhari directed work on behalf of Qaroon, whom they called 'the Honored Adham of Memphis.'

Qaroon became famous along the villages on the east riverside of the Nile, from Komombo in the south to Tennees in the north. In big villages, he built granaries and made deals with mayors to manage the business for him. He always gave the mayors bribes to ensure their cooperation and usually paid for their grains at twice the price of the market so that they wouldn't be tempted by another merchant's offer. Of course, he gave them the price for their time and effort in management of his granaries.

Some time later, Qaroon was sitting on a wooden chair in his balcony facing the Nile. His back was to Sharm, who was hunching as he awaited his master's orders.

"Are you tired, Sharm?" asked Qaroon.

"I never get tired of your service, master."

"I know," Qaroon said with a smile. "How many granaries have been built so far?"

"So far, master, we have four in the north, one in Heliopolis to the east, two in the west, and eight in the south. But why haven't you build a granary in Thebes yet?"

"Thebes is the capital of governance, the Pharaoh's city. If anyone dares to interfere in Thebes, they will see it as an invasion that would threaten their power. I prefer to stay and work away from their authorities—for now at least," he said, smiling. "What about grain collection and storage?"

"As you have ordered, we have been buying wheat, corn, lentil, beans, and malt. All the mayors are seeing to the collection and all the granaries are being filled up. But why are you storing all these grains, great one? Aren't you supposed to sell them?"

"You can be sure that I have reasons for everything I do, Sharm! Now, go get me something to eat!"

"Yes, master!" Sharm said. He bowed and walked away.

The land had dried along the Nile valley. The bones of cattle were showing under their skin. People were starving and looking in the valleys and in the vast dry lands for any green plants or bushes. The desert valleys were clear of green plants, with only thirsty yellow bushes. The desert sands had crept to the valleys and farming areas of Egypt. People from all villages and many major cities stood in long lines in front of Qaroon's granaries, taking grains for gold, silver, cattle or their own property. If they had nothing, they took grains for loans. Scribes and clerks wrote down every detail.

At the village of Ehnees, men and women stood in a long line, each waiting for their turn. Outside the granary's fence, many barefooted children were playing by the tied cattle and donkeys.

Poverty was obvious among most villagers. Mayor Samhari sat together with a clerk, who was logging down all the loans and trades of the people.

"I can't believe this," said a farmer. "It's already been three years and still no rain or floods. When will the Gods answer our prayers?"

"Thank the Gods we have Adham's granary. We would have died if he hadn't built it in Ehnees," said another farmer.

"You too? Everyone seems to think that Adham saved us all, when in reality, he was the one who did this to us."

"What are you talking about? Adham didn't cause the drought. And there's so much grain in the granary, enough for the whole village to last a few more years. Adham saved us."

"How exactly did he save us? We were fine before he came along. Yes, he provided us with food, but we have to give him everything we own in return. This is my last cow! I have to trade it for food because I don't have anything else to trade with. There's nowhere else to get food from since Adham bought all of the grains. He knew this would happen. He bought all of the food so he could sell it at the price he wants. And we were foolish enough to let him. Now we must pay the price for it."

Behind the two farmers by a few rows were too women with empty baskets. A mother and her daughter.

"If Pharaoh is a God, why doesn't he force the Nile to flood?" asked the daughter.

"He can't. There is a God responsible for the Nile, and Pharaoh cannot simply force another God to do his bidding."

"Maybe the Nile God just needs more offerings. Do we have anything we can offer the Nile God? Maybe he'll have mercy on us."

"The only thing I have left is this silver bracelet my mother gave me," the mother said. She showed her daughter a bracelet on her wrist. "I was going to give it to you. So here!" She gave her daughter the bracelet. "It is yours now, so do with it as you please!"

At the front of the line sat a clerk. He was a large man with a grim look on his face. Once he was done dealing with a villager, he would shout for the next one to come forward.

"Next!"

An old man approached with his donkey.

"What have you got for me, old man?" asked the clerk.

"I have nothing but my donkey. It's the only thing I have left to trade with."

"This donkey looks like it's about to die."

"It's all I have left. Please!"

"Fine, fine! Stop begging. I'll take your donkey under one condition. Next year you must pay double. Twenty bags of grain!"

"Why twenty?"

"This year you take ten, next year you pay back twenty. Take it or leave it."

"But this is so unfair! Who set these rules?" complained the old man.

"If you don't like what is offered, then you can go find food elsewhere. Good luck trying to find someone who will accept that corpse of a donkey. Next!"

"I'll take your deal," said the old man in a defeated tone.

"Give ten bags to this man!" shouted the clerk.

Another man wrote down the old man's name and then directed him towards the back, where he would get his ten bags of grain and hand over his skinny donkey.

CHAPTER 5

"YOU MUST STEP ON THEIR BACKS AND CRUSH THEM."

In the Pharaoh's palace in Thebes, the hall of the throne was extensively spacious. Two soldiers with lances stood still by the main door. They moved their spears apart when someone came in or went out. Many pillars rose to the high ceiling on both sides of the hall, which was lit by sunlight coming in from high windows. Fumes of burning aromatic oils come out from lanterns filling the place with the scent of comfort. The marble floor was mirror-like and glistening with cleanliness and luxury. On his throne sat Ramses, the old Pharaoh. His golden crown with a cobra on its front was shining in the indirect light of the sun. He was holding the Nile key scepter. His arms were covered with golden bracelets and his beard was leashed with golden threads. Two young female slaves were standing right behind him, moving fans made of ostrich feathers. In front of the Pharaoh, on his right and left, sat his ministers and counsellors. Right beside him sat his chief minister, Haman, on a lower chair. They were all listening to Amun's temple priest. When the priest was done, Ramses seemed troubled and pointed to the priest to go out. When he went out of the hall, Ramses looked at to the other ministers and counsellors.

"Why are you still here? Leave now! All of you!" he shouted. "Except you, Haman!"

The attendants went out while bowing to the angry Pharaoh. When the hall was emptied, Ramses took off his crown and put it aside on a chair. He wiped his bald head with his hand and rested his back on the throne, spreading his legs on the floor while Haman stood before him.

"Who is that man the priest spoke of, Haman?" asked Ramses.

"My God, he was speaking of a man from Upper Egypt who is living in Memphis. I heard about him several weeks ago and I sent inquiries about him."

"A man like that might be dangerous. We have to know who he is, where he came from, and why he's building dozens of granaries and buying almost all the grain in Egypt. Who does that? Why would someone do that? Is he challenging my authority? I want to know everything about him, Haman! Do not waste more time!"

"As you wish, my God!" Haman said as he bowed.

"I have never heard of an Egyptian who would challenge a Pharaoh. Is it possible that this man is not Egyptian? Could he be an Israelite? Maybe seeking revenge?"

"Impossible, my God! Those low animals have been created to serve you. They cannot be anything but slaves. The idea alone makes no sense."

"Bring this man to me!" Ramses demanded.

"I will, my God, but may I know what is on your mind?"

"Sit down, Haman!" Ramses said, pointing at a nearby chair. "I have just received the annual report of the Nile flood this year. It indicates that the flood coming from the Nile springs is low, maybe even lower than last year. This means that a water crisis and a drought are eminent—not just in Egypt, but in the lowlands in the East and in Abyssinia. People living in those lands, as well as the Egyptians, will suffer. And this man… What's his name?"

"Adham, Great one," replied Haman.

"Yes, this Adham is buying grains from all the valley lands and storing them in his granaries. So, in times of crisis, we will all run to him begging for food, since he will be the only one who offers it. I want this man here before the end of Thuth."

"Consider it done, my God."

"You can leave now. Tomorrow, bring me Halasi, the Nile scale director, and make him get me this month's indicators."

"As you wish, my God." Haman bowed several times and retreated to the door.

Sharm was with Qaroon in the basement of his house in Memphis. Qaroon placed three boxes in front of him. The boxes were filled with anklets and pieces of silver and gold. Sharm stood before his master with his eyes wide open but he seemed dazed and absent-minded.

"Lift this box and come with me!" Qaroon ordered.

Sharm obeyed immediately, without a word. Qaroon stepped into the next room and stopped in front of its wall.

"Open the wall!"

Sharm laid the box on the floor and pushed a big stone aside to open a hidden room behind it. Qaroon pointed to the box and Sharm lifted it and placed it inside the secret wall.

"Go get the other boxes! Quick!"

Sharm obeyed.

After moving the boxes, Sharm moved the wall back and blocked the entrance to the hidden room. They went upstairs to the hall. Qaroon looked into Sharm's eyes, and suddenly the man seemed to regain his awareness. He looked around as if he had just woken up.

"Go get me something to eat!"

Ramses was sitting down on his throne. Merenptah, his son, sat on another lower chair beside him. He had the same features of his father, the broad forehead and a high nose. He wore a pharaonic smock and a turquoise-colored head cover embroidered with golden threads.

"Merenptah, my son." Ramses paused for a moment. "I am tired."

"Do you need to rest, my Pharaoh? I can have the slaves escort you back to your chambers," Merenptah said.

"No, my son, that will not be necessary. Listen to me, Merenptah! My time as Pharaoh has come to an end."

"Of course not, Father. The temple priests will heal you. Pharaohs are above death."

"No, my son. Pharaohs are above all but death. He who controls death is truly God."

"You mean Anubis, Father?"

"If Anubis was truly God, he would shield us, the Pharaohs, from death. How many thousands of sacrifices have been presented to Anubis to protect us from death? And still, we are mortal. Anubis is not a God, my son!"

"What are you saying, Father? You will anger Anubis!"

"It doesn't matter. What really matters is that you must complete what I have started seventy years ago. Egypt has to be on the top, and we have to be on top of Egypt! He who is on the top of Egypt is on top of the world. Do you understand, Son?"

"Of course, Father. I'm going to complete your mission and you are going to see me from the afterlife."

"Tell me, Pharaoh, what are you going to do after I leave?" asked Ramses.

"I will finish building Abydos' temple and the pillars that you started in Thebes' temple."

"I know you are going to do that. I'm asking about your intentions for the slaves of Israel."

"They are filth, Father. Why do you think of them?"

"Have you heard about this deliverer that they are speaking of?"

"My glorious Pharaoh, don't believe such rumors. They are just lies that they make up to give their people hope. What you and my grandfather Seti did to them made them wish for ten deliverers, not just one." Merenptah laughed.

"What I and your grandfather did to them had a reason, my son. As you know, they supported the Hyksos, so we humiliated them and gave them every reason to fear us. You must do the same, my son. You must make your slaves fear you. Otherwise, they won't do as you say." Ramses paused for a moment and grabbed a cup to drink. "My sources have informed me that it is only a matter of time before their deliverer appears and saves them from slavery."

"Do they know who this deliverer is?" asked Merenptah.

"Not yet, but we will soon know."

The bell at the gate rang.

"Can I come in, my God?" asked Haman.

"Yes, Haman, come in!" replied Ramses.

The guards sheathed their spears, allowing Haman to step in. He bowed before the Pharaoh and his son.

"What do you have for me?" asked Ramses.

"Halasi, the Nile scale director is here."

"Let him in."

Haman went out and came back with a man holding a big papyrus roll. When the man was close to Ramses, he kneeled on the floor and kissed the Pharaoh's feet.

"So Halasi, what do you have for me today?" asked Ramses.

Halasi spread the roll on the floor and started giving Ramses his indications. Ramses was troubled by the news.

"We're going to have another dry year," said Ramses in a disappointed tone. "What about the rain in the north?"

"The same, my God. Not only in the North, but also in Sinai and in the eastern and southern mountains. It is dry across all the lands."

"Enough! You can leave now," said Ramses.

Halasi retreated while bowing. Haman bowed to the Pharaoh and started to retreat as well.

"Not you, Haman. You stay!"

"Your orders, my God."

"That man, Adham of Memphis, did you send for him?"

"I did, my God."

"I want him here next Saturday. If he is from Israel, he will not come."

"Why not?" asked Merenptah.

"They consider Saturday a holy day. They do not work, they do not go out, they do nothing. If that man is an Israelite, he will not come. Any news about the deliverer of Israel?"

"Illusions, my God! Illusions! Lies and myths. There is no prophet or a deliverer. They are giving themselves a hint of hope," said Haman.

"And how are the people of Egypt managing the drought?"

"The lands have run dry and cattle have died. The farmers' stocks have already been depleted."

"This Adham knew this would happen. He is following the footsteps of Joseph. He may have read the story."

"What story?" asked Merenptah.

"Merenptah, my son, you have so much to learn if you are to become Pharaoh. My father Seti told me about it. When the Hyksos were the rulers of Egypt, similar to today, the Nile ran dry. The king's minister was a man from Israel called Joseph. He built granaries where he stored grain for years. When the Nile ran dry, he distributed stored grain to the people, not only in Egypt, but all lands on our borders too. People from across the lands came to buy food from Egypt."

"What troubles me, my God, is that no normal Egyptian man can read hieroglyphics. If this Adham is Egyptian, how did he come by the information about Joseph?" asked Haman.

"He is either a highly educated man or an Israelite. I doubt he is educated because the people are all morons, but will find out on Saturday," said Ramses.

Many days later, the old Pharaoh, Ramses, was lying down on his bed. It seemed that the great Pharaoh was dying. Ramses' bedroom was very wide. Lanterns were lit on every wall and pillar. A huge stuffed crocodile was fixed on the wall. A golden cobra was on top of Ramses' bed. He motioned to Merenptah with his head to come closer. When he did, his father started to speak.

"Merenptah, my son. Always be on top! Never drop to the level of the people! Never become one of them! Never become normal; otherwise, they won't fear or worship you. But rule them! Conquer their hearts with fear! Make your image that of a God! Make them devoted to you! Make them worship you! Make them always in need of your approval and blessings. My son, Egypt is a gift from the Gods to us. Egypt was made a paradise for us, and we were created to rule it. During my seventy year reign as Pharaoh, never once have I heard the word 'no'. Never once has one of my wishes gone unfulfilled. My word was law, as yours shall be." Ramses paused for a moment to catch his breath. "I fought and won, I defeated and conquered, and I built and destroyed. I ruled as you will rule." He began to cough. "Few people have seen me in person. Most people have only seen my huge statues in my temples. My image in their minds is that I am enormous. To them, I am a giant, a God who should be worshiped. Never let them think for a moment that you and them are alike, or they will devour you like hungry wolves. Do anything to keep them under your feet. Do you understand?" His voice began to weaken. He was breathing with difficulty and gasping when he said his last words. "Always be on top! Always... be..."

A few days later, the huge Pharaonic solar boat was crossing the Nile to the west bank. A wooden sarcophagus was placed on board. Its cover was colored with royal colors representing Great Ramses' face. Merenptah stood still beside the sarcophagus. He was holding his father's golden scepter and had the cobra crown on his head. The new Pharaoh was surrounded by the palace's men and ministers. The long oars stroked the face of the water, adding sublimity to the funeral of the deceased Pharaoh. Amun's priests were on the other side waiting for the mummy of Ramses. Once the boat hit the sandy shore, a scaffold was suspended to the boat. Merenptah stepped off the boat first to ride on his sedan, while young priests carried Ramses' sarcophagus. As the funeral passed between the waiting priests, they all bowed to the Pharaoh. Down in Ramses' tomb, the smell of cedar wood filled the air, coming out of censers held by temple priests. Torchbearers stood up like statues holding their lit torches. When the funeral reached the main burial room, priests carried the wooden coffin and placed it in a big black marble sarcophagus while saying death prayers.

"Fly to your brothers, the Gods of immortality," said one priest.

"Pharaonic falcons, take him to the endless life," said another.

"Ramses, greatest of the greatest, master of the earth and skies, the victorious. Go back to your world and loving Gods."

Merenptah was listening and watching the burial of his father while holding the scepter in his hand. When the ceremony ended, he went back to his sedan and left on the Pharaonic sun boat.

The new Pharaoh Merenptah was on his late father's throne. He had his golden cobra crown on and was holding the Nile scepter. The guard at the door rang the bell.

"Minister Haman is asking for permission to see you," said the guard.

"Let him in!"

He adjusted his position on the throne and fixed the crown on his head. Haman entered the hall and bowed before the Pharaoh.

"Greetings and prayers to you, Great Pharaoh."

"Haman! Finally. I need you in some important matters."

"I am your servant, my God."

"How are the Egyptians doing?" asked Merenptah.

"Your greatness, people are going mad because of dryness. They are starving!"

"Is there anything that we can do for them? Have you found a solution for this drought?"

"There is nothing we can do against starvation. Hungry people will do anything to eat."

"What do you mean 'anything'?" He gave Haman a suspicious look.

"It is not their fault, my God. They are starving!"

"Haman! What happened?" Merenptah demanded.

"I didn't want to bother you with this, Great One, but since you have asked, I will tell you. Yesterday, a group of people attacked the temple. They broke the gates and they stole all the grains in the temple. When the priests stood defending the temple, they were beaten and one of them was killed."

Merenptah rolled his eyes and then looked at Haman again.

"Did you arrest the killer?"

"There were more than a hundred protesters, Great One. When the gates were broken down, hundreds broke in and pillaged the storage areas. It was absolute chaos. We couldn't know who did it."

Merenptah seemed angry but remained silent.

"I beg your pardon, Great One, but do you remember the man who your father sent for? Adham of Memphis?"

"Yes, what about him?"

"He is waiting outside in the hall. He awaits permission to see you."

"On a Saturday! Interesting. So he is not an Israelite. But my mind is very busy. I'm not in a mood to meet anyone right now."

"A thousand pardons, my God! But I suggest you meet with him. He could have the solution to our problem."

"Very well. Let him in!" Merenptah motioned with his hand.

The two guards by the gate opened the gate and a third walked in with Qaroon behind him. He wore an Egyptian smock, a head cover woven with copper threads, and leather sandals. He bowed when he stood before the Pharaoh.

"What is your story, Adham of Memphis?" asked Merenptah.

"Great one! I'm Adham, the son of Badri from M..."

"I mean how is it that an Egyptian could build all of these granaries," Merenptah interrupted. "What is the story behind that?"

"That is why I wanted to meet with you, my Pharaoh."

"I'm listening."

"My Pharaoh, you are the God of the earth and skies. You are God of Egypt and every grain of sand on its land belongs to you. Every wheat grain grows by your order and your blessing. Everything I have belongs to you. I, myself, live by your spirit." He stood up and bowed before Merenptah, who smiled and looked to Haman. "Continue!"

"Everywhere I go, I say that all my granaries and all my stored goods are only a small portion of what Pharaoh can do for Egypt. The grains I have stored can supply the whole of Egypt for another two years."

Merenptah did not comment, but motioned Qaroon to continue.

"I did not store grains by my own will. It was only by yours..."

"And we thought he is from Israel!" Merenptah said to Haman while smiling. "He is more loyal to me and Egypt than any Egyptian. Even more than some of my own counselors."

"Me? From Israel? Why, my Pharaoh? What did I do wrong? I hate those slaves with all my heart. I even hate to talk about them. That's why I did not build a granary in Goshen. I want them all to starve to death."

"It was Great Ramses who thought of this man to be from Israel. I personally rejected the thought," said Haman.

"Back to the topic at hand. You said the grains you stored are enough for two years, correct?" asked Merenptah.

"Yes, Great One."

"Very good! I am counting on you to feed the people of Egypt. You shall be Egypt's saviour. In return for your grains, you shall be well compensated from my own treasuries."

Qaroon bowed down before Merenptah.

"Haman, make sure Adham is well paid for every grain he gives."

"Yes, my God."

"You may go, Adham of Memphis!"

"Before I leave, my God, may I say something?" Qaroon asked.

"Say it!"

"My God, Egyptians are naive people. They believe anything said to them. What matters to them is to eat, drink, sleep, and live. Nothing else matters. The best way to deal with them is to make them always be in need of your blessings, to make them devote themselves to you so that they may seek your approval."

Merenptah was surprised to hear the same words he had heard from his father on his deathbed. "Continue!"

"My Pharaoh, you must force them to love you. If they don't, you must humiliate them. You must step on their backs and crush them. Great One, as long as the people's food is in your hands, they shall forever be in need of you. But some may try to rebel against you, my God! A thinking servant is a dangerous one. You must make them into non-thinking and blind followers."

"What do you mean?"

"Make opium readily available and easily accessible to them and they will forever be your blind and submissive servants."

Merenptah laughed. "I like the way you think. You are a devil in disguise, Adham. Haman, arrange a meeting tomorrow. Only you, Adham, and I shall attend. That is all for now. You can both leave." Merenptah motioned for them to go.

Haman and Qaroon retreated while bowing, and left the hall together.

"Sneaky!" Haman said. "You managed to avoid answering his question."

"What question?" Qaroon smiled.

The marketplace in Memphis was crowded as usual. A man on a donkey raised his voice, calling to the crowd.

"People of Memphis, the great Pharaoh has ordered to give each family a bag of grain. People of Memphis, a gift from your Lord the most high. You can go get it from the Memphis grain house."

People hummed happily as they rushed out of the market to Adham's grain house.

Things were a mess there. It seemed that all the people of Memphis were there to get Pharaoh's gift.

Qaroon climbed on top of the wooden gate and started shouting.

"What's going on here? What's going on?"

People quieted down as they saw him and wondered who this man could be.

"Is this how you show your gratefulness to your God for his generosity and benevolence? Stand in a line or face the wrath of the mighty Pharaoh."

People responded immediately.

While Qaroon was walking away towards his chariot, he saw a familiar face in the crowd. It was his old friend Benjamin. He was carrying a green basket and was waiting for his turn. Qaroon motioned a worker to come to him.

"Do you see that man with the green basket?" Qaroon asked, pointing at Benjamin.

"Yes, my lord," the worker replied.

"Don't give him any grains! Understood?"

"Yes, my lord."

"If he asks why, point him to me."

"Yes, my lord."

When the sun was about to set, Qaroon walked towards his chariot. Before he climbed into his carriage, a hand grabbed his shoulder.

"Qaroon!"

Qaroon turned around and saw Benjamin.

"Take your hands off me," Qaroon shouted.

"Qaroon. It's me! Benjamin!"

"Never seen you before in my life," Qaroon said. He got into his carriage and headed for the pharaonic palace in Thebes.

In the Pharaoh's palace, Merenptah lay down on a long chair and was eating a bunch of grapes. Qaroon stood before him with a sinister smile.

"My God, have you considered my request?" asked Qaroon

"You mean the gold mine east of Thebes? You are asking for a great deal, Adham."

"I don't want it for me, Great One. All the gold that we get will be yours. Every last bit of it."

"What's wrong with the current mine manager?" asked Merenptah.

"I looked over the reports that came from that mine and they were rather lacking!"

"Lacking? Are you saying the manager is stealing? This is a serious accusation, Adham," Merenptah said.

"Have a look at the reports yourself, my Pharaoh. You'll see that there is no way a mine that huge is bringing in an insignificant amount of gold like that."

"I'll have Haman investigate. If what you say is true, the mine is yours."

"You won't regret it, my God!"

Qaroon bowed in front of Merenptah.

Later that day at his house, Qaroon sat on his long chair in his balcony that had a view of the Nile. Sharm entered the room and stood before his master.

"Any orders, master?"

"I'm good for now, Sharm. You may go rest for a bit if you wish."

"Master, can I take two bags of grain?" asked Sharm, pointing at two bags in the corner of the balcony.

"I brought them for you, Sharm. Enjoy!"

"Thank you, master. Thank you!" Sharm retreated with a large smile on his face.

Some time later, Qaroon heard knocking on the door. He waited to see if Sharm would get it, but it seemed that he had fallen asleep, so he went to open the door himself. He opened the door and saw Benjamin.

"Come in, Benjamin!" Qaroon said.

"So now you know me?" Benjamin smiled and gave Qaroon a suspicious look.

"To the Egyptians, I am Adham. If they found out I was Qaroon, they would've killed me long ago."

"That's what I thought," Benjamin said. He sat down on one of the chairs in Qaroon's balcony.

"You moron! 'It's me, Benjamin?' Are you trying to get us killed? Yelling the names Benjamin and Qaroon in a place full of Egyptians?"

"My mistake!"

"You're going to need to come up with a name that won't get you killed or sold in the market."

"We'll think of that later. But right now, tell me, how did you accomplish all of this?" Benjamin asked. He marvelled at Qaroon's house and pointed at the Nile.

"I got sick of a life of slavery! I got sick of all the misery and torture that I had to endure in Goshen, so I left and worked my way up to here."

"You're not going back to Goshen?"

"Have you lost your mind? You want me to leave all of this," he pointed at the balcony of his house, "and go back to that filthy pile of donkey shit?"

"They are your people!"

"Not anymore! Speaking of which, how are those dirty slaves faring?"

"We, the dirty slaves, are fine, thanks for asking," Benjamin said in a sarcastic tone. "Everything is the same. However, the Pharaoh's men have been coming to our village more frequently to take many of the men to have them build something. There's a lot fewer men in Goshen now. And I have bad news for you."

"What?" Qaroon asked.

"It's your father."

Qaroon walked to the railing on the edge of the balcony. "Did he finally buy a cow?"

"I'm so sorry, Qaroon. Your father's dead."

Qaroon didn't turn to face Benjamin but kept looking at the Nile. "How did he die?"

"He must have fallen or tripped on something. They found him dead under the sycamore tree by the cornfield with his head bleeding out."

"What happened to my mother and sisters?"

"Both of your sisters were married but their husbands were taken by the Egyptian soldiers to help build a temple in Thebes. Your uncle Jacob has been looking after your father's herd and has been taking care of your mother and sisters."

Qaroon remained silent.

"Hearing this, have you decided to go back to Goshen and help your family? They really need you."

"They are no longer my family," Qaroon said as he turned around. "They are just slaves to me. Nothing more than that."

"But they need you!" Benjamin repeated.

"I don't need them. That is all I have to say."

They were both silent for a short while.

"Also, guess who came to visit Goshen?" Benjamin asked.

"Who?"

"Moses!"

"Who's Moses?" Qaroon asked.

"The son of Emran."

"Don't you mean Aaron?"

"No, Moses is Aaron's younger brother. To protect him from being slaughtered by the Pharaoh's men, his mother placed him in a basket and made him float away in a nearby river."

Qaroon laughed. "What? I love her logic. Your son can't get slaughtered if you drown him in the river." He pointed to his head and laughed.

"That's not all," Benjamin continued. "He came to Goshen wearing fancy Egyptian clothes. He told his family that the Pharaoh's wife found him floating in the river so she took him and raised him as her own son. After he was old enough, she told him that his real family was in Goshen, so he came back."

"Very smart man! Leave a Pharaonic palace and come to a village that smells like shit," Qaroon said in a sarcastic tone.

"I thought so too." Benjamin laughed. "I know they're his family and all, but I still don't understand why he decided to stay."

"Does he have the looks of an Egyptian prince? Or does he look like Aaron?"

"He looks exactly like Aaron. Only difference is in the way he speaks. He stutters too much, especially when he's stressed."

"Anyway, I'm glad you decided to leave Goshen too and follow in my footsteps." Qaroon smiled.

"What do you mean? I came here because my family is starving and this was the only place to get food."

"That family of yours is only stopping you from reaching your full potential. You need to let them go!"

"That's not how it works, Qaroon. Family is all I have. I can't abandon mine like you did yours."

"I know how to change your mind. Come with me to Thebes! I'll ask you then if you still want to go back to Goshen."

"What are we going to do in Thebes?" Benjamin asked.

"I'll tell you later. Let's get something to eat."

A few days later, miners were working in the burning sun of the east desert gold mine. They were wearing loincloths and wrapped their heads with white wet covers. Some of them were cutting and breaking stones and others crumbled the stones and stowed them in manual carts, which led down a midway to the ground. Pieces of stone would be washed in buckets of water to uncover gold if it was underneath. The work cycle didn't stop until night, when the workers went to sleep. They saw a chariot coming from the eastern valley. They recognized Muhebb riding on the chariot with two men. Muhebb was the Pharaoh's man in the mine. Him, Qaroon, and Benjamin were on their way to the mine. Another chariot followed. It was full of food and wine.

"Welcome, master Muhebb," said one of the mine workers.

"You can all have the rest of the day off!"

The workers all smiled. "Thank you, master!" They cheered.

"Would you like us to unload the contents of the other chariot, master?"

"If you wish! It is not for me or my guests. It is a gift from the new mine manager, Adham, to you and the rest of the workers!"

More than forty workers gathered at the entrance to the mine and thanked their new manager, Qaroon. They ate meat and drank wine. That night, they slept as they hadn't slept in years.

At night time the next day, flames were lit everywhere in the gold mine. Workers were doing their tasks in the nice weather at night. Qaroon and Benjamin were walking side by side.

"Brilliant idea, Qaroon!" said Benjamin.

"Don't call me, Qaroon." He nudged Benjamin.

"Adham! My bad... Adham!"

"You mean working at night?" asked Qaroon.

"And resting during the hot days! Genius!"

"The weather is nice. They will be more productive at night if they get rest during the day."

"What if they get restless during the day?" asked Benjamin.

Qaroon raised his eyebrows and gave Benjamin a smile.

"Oh!" said Benjamin as his eyes widened. "Opium!"

"Correct! Give them opium at the end of their shifts and they get knocked out for the day and wake up refreshed. By the way, I have a task for you!"

"What is it?" asked Benjamin.

"I don't trust the gold being refined at the Pharaoh's palace. I want it refined here in the mine."

"You want me to stay here and refine gold?"

"Better! I want you to stay here and manage the mine while I'm absent."

"I already told you, I'm here to get food for my family and then I'll head back."

"Why go back with a few bags of cheap grain when you can go back with a few bags of gold?"

"But my family..."

"Your family is holding you back from fulfilling your potential! But if you insist on helping those beggars, then please, send them your whole share of gold after you get paid. It's your decision."

Benjamin was silent for a few moments and then spoke. "I'll do it! But what are you going to do with the gold after it is refined?"

"We'll worry about that later... partner!" Qaroon smiled and extended his hand towards Benjamin.

Benjamin shook Qaroon's hand.

Merenptah was on the throne and Haman was sitting on a lower chair beside him.

"Great One, Adham is waiting outside," said Haman.

"Let him in!"

Moments later, Qaroon came in with Sharm who was carrying a wooden box. When Qaroon kneeled before the Pharaoh, Sharm placed the box on the floor and bowed.

"Where have you been, Adham?"

"I'm flattered that my God has thought of me. I was getting your highness what belongs to you!"

Qaroon motioned Sharm to open the box. In it was dozens and dozens of refined gold bars

"All of this is from the Sokkari mine?" asked Merenptah, surprised.

"Yes, my God!"

"Good! You have not disappointed me, Adham! And yet, I remain in need of your services."

"I am your servant, my God!"

"The temple granaries are empty!"

"Say no more, my God! By tomorrow morning, they will be replenished."

"And something else. People in the east, especially near Goshen, are wreaking havoc because they are starving. They are attacking and robbing Egyptian farms."

"You have not built a granary there," said Haman. "This is your Pharaoh's concern. If a granary is built there, perhaps they will stop."

"If it pleases my God, I can send some food to the people of the east in your honor," said Qaroon.

"I want you to build a granary there," said Merenptah.

"I beg your pardon, my Pharaoh! Not in Goshen! Those pigs do not deserve your divine virtue."

"I know how much you hate them, but they are our slaves and they serve the people. In these conditions, either they starve to death, or they kill more Egyptians. Both scenarios are not good for anyone. I personally enjoy having tens of thousands of slaves building things for me. If they all die off, I'll have to make the people of Egypt work instead. So do as I say and build a granary in the east."

"Surely you know better than I do, my Pharaoh! I will do as you command," Qaroon said, bowing.

"This will solve the lack of security and the developing violence problems in the east. Finish this task immediately, Adham!"

"I will, Great One! And may I have your highness' approval to go to Fayum, west of Memphis?"

"Is there any reason for this visit?" asked Merenptah.

"I would like to build a house on the river and live there!"

"Why does it have to be in Fayum?" asked Merenptah. "Why not live in Thebes, closer to the palace so that you may serve your Pharaoh?"

"I will always be at your service, Great One! If you ever need me, I will come to the palace immediately. I would just like to live in Fayum because it is more peaceful and quiet."

"Very well! Have you bought the land for the house yet?"

"Not yet, Great One!"

"Pick any land of your choosing. Consider it a gift from your Pharaoh for your loyalty and service."

Qaroon kneeled on the floor and kissed the Pharaoh's feet.

There were obvious signs of poverty and depression on all the people of Goshen. Lean children ran around to play with lean sheep in the dirty streets. The sound of flies buzzing never stopped except at night, when it was replaced by the buzzing mosquitoes. The smell of shit was everywhere. In the middle of a hot humid day, the Pharaoh's caller rose his voice in the narrow streets

"People of Goshen, go to the herb lands! Your God, the mighty Pharaoh, has blessings for you there. To the herb lands!"

The people of Goshen rushed to the herb lands. They found two rows of armed soldiers leading to a group of clerks and workers selling grains to the long line of people. At the front of the line was an old woman from Goshen.

"This is all I can offer. Will you take it or not?" complained the woman.

"This won't work," said the clerk.

"Why not? So goats are unacceptable now?"

"Your goat is either dead or dying. I can't tell the difference. I won't take your dying goat," said the clerk with a disgusted look on his face.

"We have our God!" the woman said. She turned to the people in the line behind her. "He will deliver us out of bondage and slavery!"

"Your almighty God can't even give you a healthy goat, and you expect him to save you from slavery? If you have gold, I'll take it. Silver or copper, I'll take them! But a dead goat that makes more shit than it does milk or meat? Piss off, woman!"

"God will punish you for robbing us!" she said. She took out a small silver nugget from her pocket.

The clerk nodded in approval. "Finally! You had this all along and you were offering us a corpse? Where is your bag?"

She opened the bag so the clerk could fill it with grains.

After the old woman left, he turned to the other clerk.

"Where did the old hag get a piece of silver from? Their only currencies here are shit and dead animals!"

"They probably stole it from their Egyptian masters who own the nearby lands," replied the other clerk.

"Next!" yelled the first clerk.

An old man walked up to the stand.

"Yes, old man, what have you got?"

"A goat which I cannot feed. Please, my child," pleaded the old man.

"Oh for Amun's sake! What is with all the goats? Do you filthy peasants have nothing else?"

"We have nothing because you Egyptians have everything."

"If you say so, old man. Your goat isn't as dead as the rest of them. It will give you half a bag of grain!"

"Just half?" asked the old man in a weak tone.

"Are all old people as deaf as you are? Yes, just half! You don't need that much grain anyway since you're gonna die of old age pretty soon."

"God of Abraham! Why is thou testing our belief? Where is thy salvation?" asked the old man. He raised his hands to the sky and begged his God.

"Old man! Why is thou testing my patience? Where is my damn goat?" yelled the clerk.

The old man passed the rope that was tied to the goat to the clerk, who then gave it to the second clerk.

"Go tie it with the others!"

The clerk then filled up half the old man's bag.

"Next!"

The other clerk walked to the back of the shack. It was crowded with farm animals. A few were fat but the rest were so lean that they couldn't stand. The clerk walked to the part where the goats were tied and tied the newest addition with them. He then turned towards a third clerk that was sitting in the back.

"Samy, how many do we have so far?"

"There are thirty goats, sixteen cows, and twenty sheep. Where are these going to go, Mani?"

"I heard they are going to take them to Thebes. Not sure why."

CHAPTER 6
"YOU ARE JUST LIKE ME."

Qaroon was walking around his new palace in Fayum. He was wandering around with his architect, Hoor, the one who built the palace. Hoor was a short and fat man who wore expensive Egyptian clothing but with no obvious jewelry. Qaroon had a large bottle of wine in hand with two cups on the tip of it. Hoor was describing the high pillars with lotus heads, the pharaonic trappings, and drawings everywhere and on every wall. In the corner of the vast garden, he built the slaves' residence and several workshops. The workshop for weaving linen contained a large wooden loom. Another room was for manufacturing clay pots and jars. A third workshop was for carpentry and smithing. The forth room was a huge kitchen with a slaughterhouse. Qaroon seemed fascinated with Hoor's work. There were high windows with colored glass from which the sunlight entered to enlighten the whole palace. They went downstairs to the basement.

"This safe basement is built nowhere else, Great One! Not even in Pharaonic palaces."

"I'm sure of that, my dear Hoor. How many safes have you built?" asked Qaroon.

"As you ordered, ten safes."

"How do they open? I don't see any doors."

"Their design is a new creation of mine, Great One," Hoor said proudly. He smiled.

"Where are the doors?"

"You'll see, Great One."

He stepped aside and picked an iron bar beside the wall. It was two arms long with a circular handle and a toothed broad end. It was a very large key, which Hoor struggled to carry. He inserted it in a hole in the wall and turned it inside. The wall clicked loudly and started to move to the inside on iron wheels, opening a door.

"This is the first safe," said Hoor.

They walked in the room and he picked the second key to open the second safe. Hoor lit the lantern on its wall and Qaroon opened the third door. They kept going until they were in the ninth room. Qaroon was impressed, while Hoor was proud of his work.

"How do you like your palace so far, Great One? It's unlike any I've ever built."

"A brilliant idea. Well done, Hoor. You deserve every piece of gold you got."

"Thank you, Great One," said Hoor. He bowed slightly.

"Does anybody else know about this?" asked Qaroon.

"Things done in this palace were not done elsewhere. Not even in Pharaoh's palaces. Only the workers know of this place's existence, but they have no idea what they were building, and I got different men to work on the basement, not the same ones who worked on the palace. No one knows how to get down here."

"I appreciate and admire your work, Hoor, more than you can imagine."

"Thank you, Great One. You flatter me."

"Excellent. And where is the water well?" asked Qaroon.

"In the tenth room."

Qaroon grabbed a giant key and opened the tenth room.

"Here is the water well. Even demons wouldn't know the way down here!" Hoor remarked.

"This calls for a celebration," Qaroon said. He opened the bottle of wine and started to pour some into each cup.

"Thank you, Great One." Hoor bowed again and smiled.

Qaroon handed him his cup of wine and they started to drink.

"How deep is this well, Hoor?" asked Qaroon.

"Twenty bodies deep. I dug it so deep to get pure water out of it. Would you like to taste it?"

"Yes!"

Hoor set his cup down on the edge of the well and handed Qaroon the torch. Qaroon also set his cup aside. Hoor went down two steps and threw the bucket into the well and started loosening the rope mechanism.

"You must be proud of your invention, Hoor," said Qaroon.

"Oh yes, Great One. Very!" He let down the bucket.

"It will probably bring you a fortune."

"Yes, Great One. Not a house in Egypt will go without my invention. Every soul will know the name Hoor." He laughed excitedly.

"You will probably design many new palaces like this one. Maybe even better."

"Yes, Great One!"

"Palaces better than mine?"

Hoor stopped letting down the rope.

"I'm sorry, Hoor, but I don't like that idea."

Hoor was about to turn around but Qaroon pushed him before he could. Hoor fell forward over the edge of the well but managed to grab onto the rope mechanism. He descended a couple of arms' lengths until the mechanism reached its end and he came to a stop. He was now holding onto the rope and he looked up to see Qaroon smiling down at him.

"Well done, Hoor!" Qaroon clapped. "Not only is your well beautifully designed, but it is also strong enough to withstand the weight of a fully grown fat man." He laughed.

"Great One, please!" Hoor begged. "I will burn the designs and sketches for my invention. Just please, pull me up." It was obvious that he was struggling to hold onto the rope.

"You may burn the design, Hoor, but it will never be truly erased until you are burned with it." Qaroon smiled and started to pour the wine bottle over Hoor, who was now begging for his life and screaming his lungs out.

"Almighty Ra! Save me!"

"Ra? Out of all of the Gods, why Ra? What could the God of the sun possibly do for you right now? There is no sun in here, Hoor. Can you even see the sun? Can the sun see you?" Qaroon laughed and mocked Hoor. He started to pour one of the cups of wine on him. Hoor helplessly cried for help. Qaroon grabbed the second cup from the ledge of the well.

"If I were you, I'd drink some of this delicious wine that's being wasted on your fat corpse. Why let the wine go to waste?"

Hoor started cursing Qaroon and continued to scream and beg for help.

"You know what, Hoor. I was wrong. Ra, the almighty God of the sun, has finally answered your prayers."

Hoor stopped crying and looked up at Qaroon.

"I was wrong when I told you that the sun wasn't in here. The sun is right here!" Qaroon said. He raised the torch and looked at it, smiling.

Hoor's eyes expanded in horror. Before he could say a word, Qaroon threw the torch at him. In an instant, Hoor was up in flames and screaming. The fire was so bright inside the dark well. Qaroon simply looked down onto Hoor. His eyes reflected the flames of the burning architect. It wasn't long until Hoor let go of the rope and started falling. The volume of his screams got lower and lower until Qaroon heard a thud. Hoor stopped screaming. His final echoes slowly diminished. Qaroon finally heard a splash at the bottom of the well and the fire was put out. Qaroon drank whatever was left in the cup of wine.

"Good wine should never go to waste." he smiled and started walking away in the darkness.

Sometime later, Qaroon was in his palace's basement. He had a torch lit a torch and was walking towards one of the rooms. When he went in, he lit five oil lanterns on the walls and on the central table. The room was wide, with many shelves on its walls. The table was crowded with pots, jars, and empty bottles. He stepped over to an oven and opened its door with a wet cloth. Fumes rose up in the air. He held a long metallic forceps and inserted it in the oven. He took out a hot stone plate. He placed it carefully on the table and waited for it to cool down. It contained a lump of brown powder. He used a feather to write on a papyrus paper. Off the table shelf, he picked a bottle holding a green liquid. He opened the bottle and added few drops on the brown powder while mixing with a wooden spoon. Then he opened a small rounded stone box. It contained a yellow powder. He added some of it into the mixture and continued mixing and shaking. The powder turned green. Qaroon spent some time inspecting and feeling the newly formed green powder. He went back to his papyrus notes. He laid his head on his fist while still gazing at his powder. He suddenly stood up and opened a cupboard on the wall. He got a small bottle of a red liquid. He added few drops to the powder while stirring and mixing. His eyes shone with joy as the green powder started to turn yellow. It soon turned to gold—bright, shining gold.

"I did it!" Qaroon said. He smiled. "Now I'm the richest man alive! I turned silver to gold. Soon it will be copper! Then iron! Then wood! I will even turn dust to gold!" He started to laugh.

Some time later in Heliopolis, Lamia, Helal's daughter, was coming back from the Nile after she had filled her urn with water. When she got close to her father's house, she looked behind her and saw a man following her from a distance. She stepped inside the house, put the urn down, and sat next to her father.

"Father, do you remember the man that visited us a few years ago? The one that stayed a few days and became friends with Minali?

"You mean Adham? From Memphis?" Helal asked dismissively.

"I saw him today. He was following me when I was coming back from the Nile."

Helal got up. "Are you sure it was him?"

"I think it was him, I'm not too sure."

Helal ran to the door and got out. He looked around and walked in the dirt road leading to the Nile, but there was no one there. When he returned home, his daughter was waiting for him by the door.

"What is wrong, Father?"

"Nothing. Have you seen him before today?"

"No, this was the first time since Minali disappeared. Do you think he had something to do with that?" she asked.

"I really don't know, but Minali disappeared one day after that damned man left us. Maybe he knows something."

"You can follow me tomorrow to the Nile. He might be there."

The next morning, Lamia had the urn on her shoulder and was walking towards the Nile. Helal followed her from a distance. When she arrived at the Nile shore, she stepped on a big stone and bent to the water to fill the urn. Suddenly, her feet slipped and she fell in the water. When she cried for help, Qaroon appeared from behind a tree and pulled her out of the water.

"You should be more careful!" he said.

"I slipped, I don't know how," she replied. "My leg hurts."

She uncovered her leg, which had a long scratch wound. She looked at him.

"Thank you so much! Who are you?"

"Adham. Do you remember me?"

She was silent for a few moments but then smiled. "Yes, of course! You stayed with us for a few days and became friends with Minali."

Qaroon was silent for a moment and looked at the ground as Minali's final echoes passed through his mind. He then looked at Lamia and smiled. "Yes, yes! Minali! That is exactly why I am here. To visit Minali. How is he?" Qaroon said hastily.

"Minali..."

"What is going on?" Helal interrupted. "Who is this, Lamia?"

"It's me, Adham!" Qaroon smiled.

"Adham?" Helal pretended to not remember for a second. "Adham! Son of Badri! How are you, my boy? And how is your father?"

"My father died five years ago."

"I'm really sorry to hear that," Helal said in a neutral tone.

"After that, I came to live in Memphis."

"Weren't you already living in Memphis?" asked Helal.

"I mean I bought my own house in Memphis," Qaroon said.

"And what brings you here?"

"To meet you, of course! To thank you once again for your hospitality the last time we met. And I came to see how Minali is doing. I may have a job proposition for him. I didn't know I'd be rescuing your angelic daughter on my way."

Helal looked at Lamia's wet clothes and let out a fake smile. "Let's go home to dry your wet clothes and eat something, Lamia." said Helal. "Adham, you must join us!"

"It would be a pleasure. I miss Minali and Daniali so much."

Helal gave him a suspicious look. They started walking to Helal and Lamia's house.

After going inside, Lamia placed the urn by the door and went inside. The two men sat on the platform.

"Malissa! Malissa!" Helal shouted.

Helal's wife came running in from another room. She wore a black smock and a simple hair covering. When she saw Qaroon, she hid her face with her hand.

"Come in! He's not a stranger. This is Adham, Minali's friend."

Her eyes widened and she gave Qaroon hostile looks. "Do you know where Minali is?" she asked.

"What do you mean? He isn't here? " Qaroon asked calmly.

"The last time we saw him was one day after you left."

"I last saw him one day before I left, after I thanked you all for your generous hospitality."

"Well then, where could he have gone?" Malissa asked bluntly.

"Will you get us something to eat, Malissa?" Helal intervened before Qaroon could answer.

She gave Qaroon an expressionless look and started to walk away.

"So, Adham, when did you buy that house in Memphis?"

"After my father died, I sold our sheep and goats and bought the house."

"And you haven't seen or heard from Minali since?" Helal asked in a desperate tone.

"I really wish I could be of more help. When did he disappear?"

One morning he left for Memphis to buy few goats. We haven't heard from him since.

"He may have preferred to stay in Memphis. Maybe a girl caught his eye or he felt that he could make something of himself with the goat money."

"We've considered that as well. I went through Memphis and other cities many times asking about him and just looking for him. There's no sign of him. No trace! It's as if he's disappeared off the face of the earth. The reason I'm asking you all of this is because you were the last person to talk to him before he decided to go."

"I swear to the glory of Pharaoh, I haven't seen him since I left your house."

"Where could he be?" Helal said hopelessly. He started to tear up.

"He told me that he wished to leave go to Thebes. Have you tried looking there?"

"I never heard that from him! Why would he tell you something like this and not me?" Helal said in an angry tone. "I've also been to Thebes a couple of times looking for him."

"Calm down, father Helal! I know you're angry because your son is missing and you're just looking for someone to blame because you don't want to lose hope. I'm sure one day he will return with some grandchildren for you. Then you will thank your good friend, Qaroon, for calming you down." Qaroon smiled.

"Qaroon? Who is Qaroon?" Helal asked in a suspicious tone.

Qaroon's eyes widened but he tried to remain calm. "Qaroon? Who said Qaroon? I said Amun! You will thank your good friend Amun, the God, for bringing your son back."

Helal stopped giving Qaroon a suspicious look. "The Gods don't care for us. They are Gods of the rich and the able. They have nothing to do with poor people like us."

Malissa came in carrying a tray with plates of cheese, cucumbers, and bread. Lamia followed with two cups of milk.

"What do you do in Memphis, Adham? How do you manage?" asked Helal.

"I'm a different person now, father Helal! I'm a grains trader," said Qaroon with a smile.

"Grains trader? That business is monopolized. Are there even any grains to trade in? The Nile has run dry for four years now!"

"Where do you get grains for your family, father Helal?" Qaroon asked, smiling.

"From a granary here in Heliopolis. It's owned by a man called Ad…" Helal's eyes widened and he gave Qaroon a surprised look. "You?"

"Yes, it's mine. I own granaries all across Egypt, both in the north and the south."

Helal laughed. "You're not serious, are you? Seriously, now, tell me what you do in Memphis!" Helal continued to laugh.

"I swear on my dead father, I'm not lying."

Helal's expression changed to a bitter one. "Why would you do something like this?"

"Do what, father Helal? I'm helping people through the drought!" said Qaroon.

"You are using people! You take advantage of the fact that they need you and you exploit them for gold and silver or whatever they have in their homes and hold dear. I had to give away my cattle, my wife's jewelry, and a lot of precious farming tools," Helal said angrily.

"Father Helal, we are in the middle of a crisis and I provide people with what they need. I never force anyone to buy from me," said Qaroon.

"You don't force anyone? You own all the grains of Egypt. If we don't buy from you, we starve. We are forced to buy from you."

"And what is wrong with me owning all the grain? I did what no other man could. I made something of myself," said Qaroon.

"You are not helping anyone other than yourself. Everyone knows that. Even you know that. You are just trying to justify your actions by lying to yourself and making yourself believe you're actually helping us."

"You would all starve if it wasn't for me, and no one knows what will happen next year. Suppose that the Nile dried out and the flood doesn't come! The burden on my shoulders will be twice as heavy as it is this year. I'm getting what I deserve, father Helal."

"But how did you even manage to build all of these granaries?" asked Helal. "All of the cattle in Egypt wouldn't be enough for that."

"That is a discussion for another time. I came to you for a very important matter." Qaroon smiled. "I have something to ask of you!"

"What could the richest man in Egypt possibly want of a poor farmer like me?" Helal said with a curious look.

"I want to marry your daughter, Lamia."

Helal was surprised and looked at him with a fake smile. "I haven't seen you in years and you show up at my doorstep and ask for my daughter? This is a big surprise," Helal said.

"A good surprise or a bad surprise?" Qaroon asked.

"Well, you could have asked at a better time, perhaps before I knew you were the man responsible for my family's suffering." Helal gave Qaroon a hostile look.

"You were the one who asked, father Helal." Qaroon laughed. "I'd still be your friendly sheep herding Adham if you hadn't asked me so many questions. But just pretend you didn't find out about my granaries and that I was responsible for your family's suffering. Would you consider letting me marry Lamia?"

"I have to ask her first," Helal said dismissively.

"I'm going to stay in Memphis for few days, after which I'm leaving to Fayum. I wish to hear from you before that."

"What business do you have in Fayum?" Helal asked.

"I built the greatest palace for my bride there. And I really hope that Lamia is the one to occupy it." Qaroon smiled.

"Greatest?" Helal said doubtfully.

"I made sure of that!"

"Come to me after two days. I will have an answer for you by then," Helal said as he got up.

Qaroon stood up to leave. Helal walked with him to the door. After ensuring that Qaroon had left, Helal came back to find Malissa and Lamia sitting on the platform. He sat with them and let out a long sigh.

"Have you heard what the man just said?" Helal said.

"We did!" said Malissa.

"And what do you two think?"

"I know we don't know him that well," said Helal's wife. "But he is the richest man we know. He has everything every woman dreams of! I am fine with it as long as Lamia is." She looked at her daughter.

"Weren't you just blaming him for Minali's disappearance? Now that he's rich, you're going to forget about it?" asked Helal.

"Did you notice him slip while he was talking, father?" Lamia asked. "Who is this Qaroon that he mentioned? He sounded very nervous when he was trying to cover it up."

"You are just like your father." Helal smiled. "You wouldn't let it pass! Qaroon is not an Egyptian name; it is Israelite. But why would Adham mention it—unless that isn't his real name."

"What will you do, Helal?" asked Malissa.

Helal paused for a moment and thought about what he was going to do. "Isn't he staying in Memphis for few days? I will go ask about him in the marketplace."

"Take me with you, father. I wish to go to Memphis," Lamia said excitedly.

"Prepare yourself. We are leaving in the morning."

In the middle of the crowd of Memphis' marketplace, Helal walked around with Lamia. She was overwhelmed by what she witnessed. In front of Amun's temple, there was a magician doing tricks in the middle of a crowd that surrounded him. He threw his stick on the ground and turned it to a cobra. People were dazzled by the magician and clapped for him many times. While Lamia was watching the magician, Helal poked her to look at Qaroon who entered the market on his sedan. They stared at him from a distance. The slaves put down the sedan on the ground before the slaves' market. Qaroon stepped out of it and started walking among the crowd. He was wearing his Egyptian clothes and head covering. His golden bracelets and necklace shined in the sun. He was walking towards a slave auction with Sharm following him. Helal and Lamia were walking behind him at a distance, where he could not see them should he turn around. Helal then motioned Lamia to stop and they both moved to the side of the road and hid behind a crowd.

"Qaroon!" Helal shouted. "Qaroon!"

Qaroon turned around to see who was calling him. When he saw no one, he thought it was just his imagination so he turned around and continued walking.

"We've seen enough," Helal told Lamia. "Let's go!" Helal grabbed his daughter's hand and started walking away from the market.

A day later, the sky was cloudy and the land was dry. There wasn't a single green bush growing in Helal's field. Only a few yellow onion sprouts grew beside the reed hut. Helal was sitting under a big sycamore tree looking at a figure that was approaching from a distance. After the figure was closer, he recognized the expensive clothing and the fancy jewels. It was Qaroon.

"Fine day, isn't it, father Helal?" asked Qaroon with a smile.

"Fine day? My lands are dry, all my cattle have either died or have been sold, my family is hungry, and I can do nothing about it. The only thing that managed to survive the drought is this sycamore tree because it can withstand dryness for quite a long time. Fine day you say!" Helal looked at the ground.

"I know things aren't going so well because of the drought, but I'm sure they will get better," Qaroon replied.

"This is all your fault! Do you think this is the first drought we've had? In my entire life, I've experienced many droughts and never before have I suffered this much."

"Father, Helal, when we become a family, I will look after you of course and make sure that all your needs are met."

"It's not just me! It's people all across the land. You made them suffer a great deal. Helping me and my family does not do them justice."

"Then what will you have me do? Give them food for free? Donate the fortune that I earned through hard work and sweat?" Qaroon asked.

"Of course not! But give the grains and the crops back to the common people and the farmers! This monopoly of yours is ruining lives. You've had your fun. You have enough gold to last you hundreds of lifetimes."

"I'm sorry, father Helal, but what I do with my gold or my lands or my possessions is my business," Qaroon said in an irritated tone.

"Never in my life have I met someone so selfish and so inconsiderate of others," Helal said as he shook his head.

"And you think you're such a self-sacrificing saint?" Qaroon asked. "You think you're a selfless and considerate man?" he continued.

"I'm not claiming to be a saint, but I am not a selfish man. I would gladly help those who are in need of my help. Unlike you." said Helal.

"You are just like me. The only difference is that you've never been given the opportunity to show the world your true form—the greed infested side that exists within all of us that is riddled with self-love and envy of those who have what we don't."

Helal was about to speak but Qaroon continued.

"Do you have any idea how many poor people out there need your help? Do you have any idea how many of them wish they had a fraction of what you have? Have you ever helped them?"

"I would if I could."

"But that's where you're wrong, father Helal. You can help them! You just don't want to. You make up the excuse that you can't and you end up believing your own lies." Qaroon paused for a moment. "Before you say anything, answer just one question: If there was a person who had nothing, would you trade lives with them? They would be forever happy because of you but you would suffer."

Helal remained silent and looked at the ground.

"Would you at least give them half of what you own?"

Helal did not reply.

"That's what I thought," Qaroon said. "You are willing to help others, but not at the cost of your own suffering. You put your own self-interest above that of others. You are just as selfish as I am."

"In that case, Qaroon, I believe you marrying my daughter is out of the question."

Qaroon's eyes widened and he was silent for a brief moment. "Who is Qaroon?" he asked in a shaky voice.

"Enough of this, Qaroon! I know who you are!"

Qaroon did not answer.

"Where is Minali?" Helal demanded. "Where is my son?"

"I don't know where Minali is!"

"You expect me to believe that after all the lies you've told? I want to know where my son is so I can at least bury him if he's dead," Helal said in a desperate voice before starting to tear up.

Qaroon waited for a few moments. "Will you tell anyone who I am?"

"I know doing so will get you killed, so no! And I will also tell Lamia not to tell anyone," Helal looked at Qaroon. "But if I ever see you again, if you ever come near my daughter again or step foot near my home or my family, I will make sure the whole of Egypt knows who you are."

"Can I trust that you will keep your word?"

"I am a man of my word! That used to mean something before the world got infested with greed, lies, and deceit. I've known who you were for a day now. If my intention was to tell everyone, you would be dead by now because even your own slaves would turn on you."

Qaroon was silent. He was about to say something.

"I believe you've said enough, Qaroon!" Helal interrupted and looked to the side.

Qaroon stood still for a few moments and then turned around and started walking away.

CHAPTER 7

"You will always be a slave!"

Merenptah was sitting on his throne. He seemed to be angry with Haman, who stood fearfully before the Pharaoh.

"You were the one who told my father that he was to be trusted!" Merenptah shouted at Haman.

Haman bowed before the Pharaoh in fear and kept his head down. "God of the earth and skies, don't be upset! He is on his way over here right now and we'll know the whole story when he gets here," Haman said in a trembling voice.

"I can't believe that one of those filthy slaves has deceived us. This is your fault, Haman. It was you who said that it was impossible."

"But my God, he was so good an actor that all of us believed him."

He was interrupted by the sound of the guard's lance on the floor announcing the arrival of Qaroon. Merenptah motioned the guards to let him in. Qaroon came in and bowed before the Pharaoh. He kneeled on the floor in front of Merenptah.

"My God has summoned me and I am at my God's disposal."

"What is this that we've heard, Qaroon?" asked Haman.

Qaroon was shocked to hear his real name. He tried to think of an excuse but could not. He did not get up but remained on his knees in front of Merenptah with his head facing the ground.

Merenptah's face turned red. "How dare you think that you could lie to me?" he shouted.

"How did my Pharaoh find out?" Qaroon asked while still kneeling.

"We caught one of your men at the mine stealing gold," Haman said in a neutral tone. "After some 'persuasion' we made him talk," Haman smiled.

"Benjamin?" Qaroon looked at Haman.

"Yes, Benjamin." Haman turned to Merenptah. "God of the earth and skies, this man is clearly guilty of deceiving and lying to his Pharaoh. His life is at your mercy, my God!"

"My God, am I allowed to speak?" Qaroon asked.

Merenptah looked to Haman for advice.

"He will say anything to save his life, my God," Haman said in a dismissive tone.

Merenptah contemplated for a few moments. "Let's hear it!"

Qaroon stood up to face the Pharaoh. "I ask my God for forgiveness. I can explain why I did what I did. Every man chooses a God for himself. Those damned Israelites chose to worship a God they do not see. A false glimmer of hope to get saved from slavery that they exaggerated and made into an entire religion. I, however, chose to worship you, my God! You are a God in the body of a man and you deserve to be worshipped because you walk among us and bestow your blessings upon us. I resented the people of Israel and their false God and accepted you! I have told you before that everything I own, including my life, is yours. I only lied about my name because I didn't think the God of Egypt, Merenptah, would accept a filthy slave to worship him, so I pretended to be an Egyptian so I can worship you and serve you in peace without the fear of getting slaughtered in my sleep. What I have done in Egypt in the past five years, I did it while I was praying in your temples, kneeling under your feet, and seeking your gratification. My success is a proof of your gratification. All

I have been doing, I have been doing for you, my God." he said while bowing.

Merenptah looked pleased while Haman was throwing hostile looks at Qaroon.

Qaroon stood up again. "I obeyed my God's command by building a granary in Goshen, even though I would have preferred that they starve to death. My God, it is not my fault that I was born one of the people that I despise so much. I am at your mercy, my God! My life is yours should you choose to take it and it is also yours should you choose to spare it!" Qaroon bowed before Merenptah.

Merenptah seemed satisfied with Qaroon's defence. He looked to Haman, who did not seem very convinced.

"My God, as I've told you, he will say anything to save his life, including lie to you as he did before," Haman said in an angry tone.

"Nonsense. Haman, this man here is an Egyptian trapped in the body of a slave. Unlike the traitor Moses. Imagine you were born an Israelite, Haman, would you not choose to worship me instead of the false God of Israel?" Merenptah asked Haman.

"Of course, my God! But..."

"But what, Haman?" Merenptah asked while giving Haman a stern look.

"Nothing, my God! I beg for your mercy and forgiveness. Now, to the matter at hand. The matter of Benjamin's punishment," said Haman.

Merenptah turned to Qaroon. "I have good news for you, Adham! You will be the one to decide what punishment Benjamin deserves."

Qaroon smiled. "You will not regret this decision, my God!" He got down to his knees and started kissing Merenptah's feet again.

Merenptah motioned Haman and Qaroon to leave and they started retreating backwards while bowing.

After the doors were closed behind them, Haman turned to Qaroon.

"You may have him fooled, but I can see right through you, Qaroon!" Haman said with a hostile look on his face.

"And I can see right through you, Haman!" Qaroon smiled. "A deceitful liar who compliments and flatters a Pharaoh to stay at their feet and take advantage of them. A hypocrite! Not very different from the rest of us."

"What do you mean by that? I serve my Pharaoh because I love to serve my Pharaoh!"

"Then would you be fine with me going to our Pharaoh and telling him that you are so devoted to his service that you are willing to work for him and offer your services and expertise free of charge? I'm sure our Pharaoh will love that idea! And I'm sure you will be even happier because you do this out of your love for your Pharaoh and not for the love of gold... correct?"

Haman remained silent.

"Well then, could you please direct me to the dungeons so that I may see my friend Benjamin?" Qaroon asked.

Down in the dungeons, two massive Anubis statues made of marble stood at each end of a large gate. Two guards were standing still with their lances guarding the gate. The large gate had two keyholes in the center. The echoes of whipping and screaming could be heard from inside the gate. Nothing could be seen on the other side, as it was too dark. Haman and Qaroon came down a long set of stairs. Haman was holding a torch.

"Let us through!" Haman ordered.

The guards moved their spears out of the way and placed them on the side. Each guard took a key set off his belt and inserted it into the keyhole on his side. They then pushed the gates open and Qaroon and Haman walked through with one of the guards following them. The echoes of the screams and lashes became louder. It was a narrow corridor compared to the rest of the palace's corridors, and it had dozens of cells on each side. The smell wasn't pleasant. There was a worker walking in the corridors and sliding food to certain prisoners from under the doors. Haman stopped.

"Guard! Unlock this cell!" Haman ordered.

The guard obeyed and unlocked the cell. The cell was dark on the inside. It had a small window that let in little sunlight. At night time, the dungeons were pitch black. A real nightmare for the prisoners. Benjamin was tied to a wooden cross.

"Water!" Benjamin said faintly. "I need water!"

"How long has he been here?" Qaroon asked.

"Three days!" answered the guard.

"That will be all!" Haman motioned the guard to leave.

"Will you be needing the key to the cell?" the guard asked.

Haman looked at Qaroon.

"This cell will be vacant before I leave, so no, I don't need the key. What I do need is a mallet and a few nails!"

"How many would you like, my lord?" the guard asked.

"Bring me a handful! Any size will be fine. And a bucket of water!"

"Your orders, my lord!" The guard left.

"I am going go back up! I'm not enjoying the smell of open wounds and rotting flesh or the sound of people screaming," Haman told Qaroon while handing him the torch.

Qaroon did not reply and Haman walked away. Qaroon walked into the cell and lit a lantern that was on the side of the cell. Benjamin was barely conscious and his head was facing the floor of the cell.

"Water!" Benjamin said in a frail voice. "Please!"

"Water will be here shortly!" said Qaroon.

Benjamin raised his head to look at the person in his cell.

"Qaroon?" Benjamin regained some of his consciousness.

"Yes, Benjamin!"

"Are you here to set me free?" Benjamin asked.

"Set you free?" Qaroon mocked him. "What gave you that idea?"

"Because you are my friend!"

"I was your friend, Benjamin. Until you betrayed me! You stole gold from behind my back and you told everyone who I really am. It was only a miracle that my head didn't get cut off."

"Qaroon, I'm sorry!" Benjamin cried. "They tortured me. I had to!"

"That part I understand. But what I don't understand is why you would steal from behind my back. After all I've done for you?" Qaroon shouted at Benjamin.

"My family was..."

"Don't you dare tell me about your family!" Qaroon interrupted. "With what I was paying you, you could have easily fed all of Goshen. You were making more gold than all of our ancestors combined. But that wasn't enough!"

"I'm sorry!" Benjamin cried. "I got greedy! I just wanted more and I couldn't resist." He started sobbing.

"Merenptah nearly killed me because of you! My identity was almost compromised to the public and I would've lost everything! You're sorry? How does that help me?"

The sound of footsteps grew louder. Moments after, the guard returned with what Qaroon asked for.

"A bucket of water, a mallet, and a handful of nails," the guard said. He put the bucket on the floor and handed Qaroon a small tray with a mallet and about nine nails, which were about the size of a finger.

"Give me your whip!" Qaroon demanded.

The guard reached for a small whip that was rolled up and tied to his belt. He handed it to Qaroon.

"That will be all!" Qaroon motioned the guard to leave.

The guard walked away.

"Qaroon, please!" Benjamin stopped crying and started begging.

Qaroon threw the whip on the floor and walked towards the bucket. There was a cup inside it. Qaroon filled it up and walked towards Benjamin.

"Didn't you at first refuse to work with me because you said your family needed you? And that you're going to work with me so that you can feed them? How much gold did you send your family?" Qaroon asked.

"Nothing!" Benjamin said in a sad tone. He looked at the floor in shame.

Qaroon extended the cup to Benjamin's mouth and let him drink. Benjamin drank the water like a mad man until he finished what was in the cup.

"Do you believe in God, Benjamin?" Qaroon said. He walked towards the bucket to fill up the cup again.

"Of course I do!"

Qaroon paused for a moment. "I'll tell you why the idea of God is absurd!"

Qaroon made Benjamin drink the second cup of water.

"The God that you worship is unfair! Unkind! Cruel and without remorse! He rewards the non-believers such as the Egyptians with wealth, power, and superiority over others, and he punishes the people who believe in him like the Israelites who have now been slaves of the Egyptians for centuries. Unlike the Pharaoh of Egypt! Loyalty to the Pharaoh gets you gold and riches beyond imagination. Tell me, Benjamin, is it not strange that out of the whole of Goshen, I am the only one who managed to escape from that poor pile of donkey shit while the rest of you who pray to your God for salvation are still rotting there and are no more than cattle to the Egyptians?" Qaroon asked.

Benjamin remained quiet.

"Why does God favour the Egyptians? Why does he favour the non-believers while his supposed loyal slaves rot? I'll tell you why! It's because he doesn't exist! And if he did exist, then he really isn't as merciful or as kind as people say he is. He is just an evil being who is having fun! Playing with us! Testing us! If that were true, I really understand his point of view. There really isn't that much fun in having world peace where every person alive worships you. You need to have some chaos. Some disorder. Blood, massacres, greed, deceit, genocides, slavery, thievery, adultery, envy… That sounds a lot more exciting than loyal slaves who devote their lives to you, don't you think?"

Benjamin was just looking at Qaroon with scared eyes.

Qaroon took a few steps back and grabbed the mallet and a few nails. He then started slowly walking towards Benjamin.

"That is exactly what the world is like; humans fighting against each other! What they fight for doesn't matter—whether they wage wars for land, riches, religion, or politics, or even if it's just a drunken brawl, it doesn't matter. In the end, the fight must continue. And I don't plan on being a casualty in this fight! I plan on making as many casualties as necessary to keep on surviving. And by survival, I don't mean to continue breathing. I mean to live! To live a full and luxurious life with as much power and possessions as possible. I'll kill any living creature that gets in my way! And unfortunately, Benjamin..." Qaroon raised the nail in front of Benjamin's tied hand. "You got in my way!"

Qaroon raised the mallet and struck the nail into Benjamin's hand. Benjamin's scream echoed in the dungeons and made its way up the staircase leading out of the dungeons, making anyone who was passing by the stairway hear his anguish.

"Where is your God now?" Qaroon shouted as he struck the mallet a second time on the nail, which went through Benjamin's hand entirely and started piercing through the wood.

"Goddamn you, you bastard!" Benjamin said while he screamed.

Qaroon laughed. "The only one being damned is you, Benjamin," Qaroon said. He struck the nail a third time. "Where is your God now? Where was your God when your people were getting whipped, tortured, and raped for the last few centuries?" Qaroon struck the nail a fourth time. "Either he isn't there at all!" He struck it a fifth time. "Or he's just watching you suffer and laughing at you."

Benjamin's screams didn't stop for a second. Blood was dripping down his hand and making a pool on the floor.

"You're overreacting, Benjamin! We're still on the first nail." Qaroon smiled.

"Qaroon, please! I beg you!" Benjamin cried.

"The same way you beg God?" Qaroon asked. "There is a greater chance of me sparing your life than God striking me down or setting you free."

"I'll do anything you want! I'll give you anything you want!" Benjamin continued crying.

"What can a filthy slave like you offer me, Benjamin? You have nothing."

"I'll do anything you want!" Benjamin said desperately.

"Will you make me your God?" Qaroon said in a sarcastic tone.

"Yes, anything!"

"Will you worship me and do whatever I ask of you?"

"Yes, just please, let me go!"

"Let me tell you something, Benjamin. I am more of a God than your God! Your life is at my mercy! I can choose to spare you or kill you. But your God doesn't care! He's just watching you from above and laughing at you!"

Benjamin was trembling and sobbing. Qaroon walked over to Benjamin's second hand and struck a nail into it. The same screams and the same echoes were heard. After the nail had pierced through the wood, Qaroon stopped striking it.

"You know what, Benjamin? I'm prepared to show you mercy!"

Benjamin stopped sobbing and looked at Qaroon.

"I have a proposition for you. You become my slave! I will be your Egyptian master and you will do everything I say. Only then will I consider sparing your life." Qaroon smiled.

Benjamin raised his head and gave Qaroon a hateful look. "You're not an Egyptian!" he said bitterly.

"I am an Egyptian! I can prove it!" Qaroon threw the mallet and nails and grabbed the whip from off the floor. "You're a slave and deserve to be whipped for disobedience." Qaroon laughed. "I'm the Egyptian who's going to whip you!"

"You're no less a slave than I am!" Benjamin muttered.

Qaroon paused for a moment. He then raised his arm back and whipped Benjamin on the chest. Benjamin screamed and continued to scream as Qaroon whipped him continuously. Benjamin's flesh was starting to peel off with every lash he received and blood started to drip down his chest.

"You're a slave, Qaroon!" Benjamin screamed. "You will always be a slave!"

Qaroon did not reply but started viciously whipping Benjamin harder with each lash. Qaroon's facial expression showed hatred.

Benjamin's screams were continuous until eventually, they stopped when he fell unconscious. Qaroon continued whipping the unconscious Benjamin a few more times until he grew tired.

"Guard!" Qaroon shouted.

The guard's fast paced footsteps could be heard coming closer until the guard walked into the cell. He saw that Benjamin's chest was completely drenched in blood and there were two pools under each of his hands.

"Your orders, my lord?" the guard asked.

"Bring me a bottle of wine! I need it now!" Qaroon ordered.

"Yes, my lord!" the guard said. He withdrew and rushed to get a bottle of wine.

Qaroon threw the whip and grabbed the cup of water. He filled it up and drank it. Shortly after, the guard returned with a bottle of wine and a cup. Qaroon opened the wine and dismissed the guard. After pouring the wine in the bottle, he sat down. The dungeon was quiet, to the point that Qaroon could hear the unconscious Benjamin breathing. Qaroon finished his cup and then poured another. Before drinking it, he got up and poured wine on Benjamin. This didn't wake him up. Qaroon reached for the torch. He slowly approached Benjamin with a grim look on his face. When the torch was next to Benjamin's body, Qaroon looked at him. His expression turned to regret when he saw the blood dripping from his hands and the peeled skin on his chest. Qaroon paused for a moment and hesitated. He teared up and turned around.

"Why, Benjamin?" Qaroon cried. "Why?"

Qaroon threw the torch on the ground and went to grab his cup of wine. He grabbed it and drank it all while facing the wall. Qaroon felt heat emitting from behind him so he turned around immediately and saw that the wine that had dripped on the floor had caught a fire from the torch. Before Qaroon could react, Benjamin was set on fire.

"Benjamin!" Qaroon screamed.

Benjamin was awoken immediately and his screams started again. But this time, the screams were much louder. They were the screams of a man whose flesh was being burned while he still breathes. Qaroon grabbed the bucket of water and splashed it all over Benjamin, but the fire was not put out. His screams continued while Qaroon's eyes were lit with the reflection of his burning childhood friend.

"Benjamin!" Qaroon cried.

The guard came running into the cell. He stared at the burning Benjamin with horror. The smell of burning flesh was starting to fill the room. Qaroon walked over to the guard, grabbed his lance, and stabbed Benjamin in the left side of his chest. Benjamin's screams were instantly silenced.

"Put out the fire," Qaroon ordered in a weak voice. "Now!" Qaroon shouted.

The guard ran out of the cell.

"Fire!" shouted the guard. "We have a fire! Get the water buckets!"

It wasn't long until a few guards came rushing in with water buckets and the fire was put out. Qaroon got down on his knees.

"Benjamin!" Qaroon cried. "I'm sorry!"

He stayed that way for some time. The smell of Benjamin's burned corpse had flooded the dungeons. Qaroon got up and put a neutral expression on his face.

"Bury his body!" Qaroon ordered the guard who was standing by the door.

"Your orders, my lord!"

Qaroon walked away.

A few weeks later, Qaroon sat on his chair having his dinner in the dining hall of his palace. Three men were serving him. The first was presenting food, the second poured wine in his cup, and the third stood by him describing the food.

"This is an Egyptian goose, master. It is has been in the oven since yesterday, so you can imagine how perfectly cooked the meat will be."

The second slave cut the goose leg and put it in front of Qaroon, who looked at it with excitement. It wasn't long until he started eating it and drinking wine.

"Give me the rest of it!" said Qaroon.

The cook tore the goose apart and put it in his master's plate. The other slave filled his cup with wine.

"This grape wine is one year old, master."

Qaroon drank all the wine from the cup and burped loudly, then he put his hands on his stomach and stretched his back on the chair.

"Where is Sharm? Go get him!" he ordered the slaves.

One slave went to fetch Sharm, while the others waited by their master's side. After Sharm came in, Qaroon grabbed the bottle of wine and motioned Sharm to follow him into the balcony. The other two slaves started to clean up the table. In the balcony, he lay down on his long chair and drank half of the bottle. Sharm stood by his side.

"Your orders, master," said Sharm.

"What did you do with the girl that I bought yesterday?" Qaroon asked.

"She is ready and waiting for you in the third bedroom wearing the clothes you bought."

"She is beautiful, isn't she?"

"If you say so, master."

"Come closer, Sharm," Qaroon ordered.

Sharm came closer and Qaroon stood up to face him. He gave him a sharp look. Sharm's body relaxed and his eyes were wide open.

"Take the basement key, go down stairs, and in front of my room there are two boxes on the floor. Carry them to the third safe, close the doors, and come back to me. Go!" Qaroon ordered.

Sharm obeyed his master with a bow and walked away.

Down in the basement, Sharm walked in the hall holding a torch in his left hand and a big iron key in his right. He was walking calmly, for he was still enchanted. In the basement, he saw the two wooden boxes on the floor. He opened the first safe, then the second and the third. He went back to the boxes. He carried the first one on his shoulder, walked through the first door, again, then the second and then the third. He placed it on top of other boxes beside the wall. He went back to bring the second box. While he was carrying the second box, the box bumped into the edge of the gate and it fell. The box was shattered into pieces and its contents of golden nuggets spread on the floor. The sound of the crash shocked Sharm. He started panicking and looking around him.

"Where am I? What is this? What is all this gold?" Sharm said, astonished.

Upstairs, Qaroon was walking next to the hidden entrance and heard the sound of the box crashing so he rushed downstairs to where Sharm was. When he got there, he saw Sharm on his knees collecting gold nuggets and placing them back in the broken box. He seemed very happy.

"Sharm!" Qaroon shouted.

Sharm was startled. He got up quickly and turned to Qaroon. "Master! What is all this gold? I don't know how I got here or where I am, I just found myself waking up to all this gold falling on the ground!"

"It's okay, Sharm! I'll explain everything. Just come closer!"

Sharm obeyed and walked closer. After Qaroon gave him sharp gaze, Sharm did not seem to be enchanted.

"You will remember nothing of what happened today. You will forget about the gold that you just saw. Understood?"

"Yes, master," Sharm said neutrally with a nod.

"Follow me," Qaroon told Sharm. He started to walk out of the basement.

Sharm followed.

A few days later, Qaroon was having his breakfast while Sharm was standing by his side.

"So, Sharm. Tell me what you did two days ago!"

"I'm honestly not sure, master. I can't remember a single detail from that day."

"That's strange. Are you sure?" Qaroon gave Sharm a doubtful look.

"Yes, master! Why would I lie to you?"

Qaroon gave him a suspicious look and grabbed a bunch of grapes. He ate some of them and gave Sharm the rest.

"Take these, Sharm!" he said with a smile.

Sharm accepted the grapes with a smile.

"Now, you are going to take the chariot and go to my granary in Ehnees. Bring Mayor Samhari and come back to me," Qaroon ordered.

"Master, I returned from Ehnees five days ago. Why go again so soon?"

"Watch yourself, Sharm! Don't question my orders! But because I'm in a good mood, I will tell you that this year, people are paying back what they owe from the last few years. Since the Nile has been kind and the floods have been plenty, I imagine they'll have enough to pay back the loan. Now go!" Qaroon ordered.

"Yes, master!" Sharm retreated with a bow.

"Don't forget to tell him to bring the debt charts with him."

Qaroon could see Sharm leaving on the chariot from the balcony. After he left, Qaroon went downstairs and headed to the slaves' residence.

Ram, one of his slaves, walked up to him.

"Your orders, master," said the slave obediently.

"Nothing right now. Get back to your work," Qaroon ordered.

The slave returned to the workshop and Qaroon walked to Sharm's room. He opened the door and went in. Inside the room was a mess and Qaroon started to search the room. He lifted the bed cover to find a wooden plate. He removed the plate and there was a bag under it. When he opened it, he was shocked. It was full of gold nuggets and jewels.

"That backstabbing son of a whore! After all I've done for him," Qaroon said while shaking his head. "Ram! Ram!"

Ram came running in.

"Your orders, master."

Qaroon walked up to him and gave him a sharp look in his eyes. His arms dangled beside him and his head relaxed with his eyes wide open.

"Carry this bag and follow me," Qaroon ordered.

Ram did as his master ordered.

The next morning, Qaroon was resting on his long chair with Sharm standing next to him.

"Sharm, I have a problem and I'm not sure if you can help me with it."

"I'll do anything for you, master. You just need to say the word."

"Can you keep a secret?"

"Of course, master. I am your loyal slave."

"Of course you are." Qaroon gave him a fake smile. "Follow me."

Sharm followed Qaroon to the basement.

"I didn't know we had a room down here, master." said Sharm while pretending to be surprised.

"That is why it is a secret."

"What kind of problem would you like me to help with, master?" Sharm asked.

"There is a big snake in here and I would like you to kill it for me."

"Of course, master."

Sharm continued following Qaroon and did as he ordered. Qaroon opened the first safe door to show Sharm and Sharm opened the rest of the safe doors. They walked through them. As Sharm opened the rusty tenth door, it squeaked loudly. Qaroon stepped downstairs towards the well and Sharm followed.

"The snake is down there!" said Qaroon.

Sharm approached the well's ledge and leaned forward.

"Can you see the snake, Sharm? It's really big."

"No, master," replied Sharm.

"I'm looking right at it," Qaroon said, before pushing Sharm forward over the ledge of the well. He was very heavy and it took Qaroon a lot of force to manage it. Sharm didn't even have time to scream or shout because his head hit the ledge on the other side of the well. Qaroon was expecting a splash, but he instead heard a thud. Sharm's body crashed to the bottom of the now dry well.

"A big snake indeed!" Qaroon said in a disappointed tone. "You keep feeding it until it grows, then it turns on you!"

CHAPTER 8
"BUT I HAVE TO BE!"

The drought had ended and the river was flooding. Helal's field was covered with golden wheat. It was almost time for harvesting. Helal and his son-in-law, Basmi, arrived at the field, each riding a donkey. They were on their way to Qaroon's granary in Heliopolis. Basmi's donkey had four large bags of grains on its back.

"Basmi, I have grown old," said Helal.

"You are still young, father Helal. When people see you with Lamia, they think you are her brother." Basmi smiled.

Helal smiled. "Are you happy with Lamia, Basmi?"

"I'm very happy! You have raised your daughter to be an excellent wife, and she will make an amazing mother," Basmi replied.

"I wish you two all the happiness in the world."

They continued riding their donkeys until they reached the granary. Although it was early in the morning, there were still many people there. They were all there to pay their debts for the previous years. Helal and Basmi went to stand in line.

"All these people came to pay back their debts?" Basmi wondered.

"It is more crowded than last year. I imagine Adham must be happy!"

"You mean Qaroon?" Basmi asked.

"I'm sorry?" Helal was surprised.

"You haven't heard? It turns out the Adham that owns all of the granaries in Egypt is actually an Israelite named Qaroon."

"How do you know this?"

"My friend's uncle's wife's sister has a son who works in the Pharaonic palace. He told her that a friend of his, who's a guard, overheard the Pharaoh confronting Adham about his identity as Qaroon, and that Qaroon admitted to being an Israelite. The rumors spread quickly from the palace guards to their families and I don't think it will be long before the whole of Egypt hears the news."

"How long ago did you hear this?" Helal asked.

"About two days ago. Why?"

"I imagine that once the people here about this, they won't be too pleased that an Israelite owns all the granaries in Egypt and is the main cause of their suffering."

"What do you think they'll do?" Basmi asked.

"If the Pharaoh doesn't do something about it, they will storm Qaroon's palace, kill him, raid and pillage his treasures and burn his palace to the ground."

"Once Qaroon hears that his identity has been compromised, it would be wise of him to gather what he can and leave Egypt."

It was almost their turn in line.

"The line is going by a lot faster than I expected."

"Last year we were all begging for compassion and we were willing to do anything to get food. We haggled, bargained, and took our time to trade with whatever we could. But this year there is no drought. Every farmer here harvested crops and is able to repay their debts. So they just show up, pay what they owe, and leave."

"Next!" shouted the clerk, who was sitting on a wooden chair behind a small shack.

Basmi and Helal carried the four bags and walked forward to the clerk.

"Names and what is owed," demanded the clerk.

"Helal and Basmi. We took six bags of grains last year and we are here to give back four."

"When do you think you'll be able to pay back the other eight?" The clerk said, looking at his debt sheet.

"By the end of the season, I'll have all eight bags here."

"Very well!" The clerk checked their names on his sheet and wrote down what they owed. "You can give those four bags to my colleague over there." He pointed to his right where a worker was stacking bags of grain. "Next!"

Helal and Basmi walked over to the second clerk. Behind them was a man with no bags of grain. He walked up to the clerk.

"Name and how much was owed?"

"Hassan from the nearby farm. I borrowed two bags of grain last year," said the man.

"Are you here to pay the loan back or ask for an extension?" the clerk said, looking at his debt sheet.

"I'm here to pay but I only have silver."

"Very well." The clerk made some calculations on a sheet of paper. "This is how much you owe," he said, showing the man.

The man gave the clerk what was owed and left. Helal and Basmi handed over the four bags to the other clerk and were also on their way.

Qaroon was taking a walk in his palace. When he entered the gardens, he saw smoke coming out of a chimney. The only chimney near the gardens came out of his lab oven in the basement.

"This soon?" he said while smiling.

He ran to the oven in the basement lab. He waited for all the smoke to clear out and for the oven to cool down a bit, then he took a black stone plate out of the oven. The plate's top surface was regularly divided into templates, each is the size of a nugget. These templates were filled with a brown powder. He smiled and walked over to a nearby table that had glass and clay bottles containing many chemicals. He then grabbed a few of the bottles and started mixing precise amounts of certain chemicals into an empty bottle. The result was a transparent dark green liquid. He poured it over the brown powder and waited for it to absorb all the liquid. He stared at the plate in front of him for a long while. His attention did not divert. He had a mild smile on his face, which became wider and wider when the brown powder started to turn yellow. He then got up, turned the plate upside down, grabbed a hammer, and struck it on the back. Pieces of gold fell to the floor. He placed the plate on the table and got down on his knees to inspect the gold. He grabbed one nugget and his smile widened again.

After gathering all the nuggets and placing them in a box, he walked over to the table and started mixing chemicals and powders again to form the same brown powder. He then filled each slot on the plate with this powder and placed the plate in the oven.

A chariot led by six horses was rushing down a long road headed to Goshen. It was now in a familiar place. It was next to the cornfield that used to belong to the Egyptian farmer that Qaroon killed with the axe. The horses were running fast and the chariot was almost at its destination. They were now next to a large withered sycamore tree.

"Stop!" Qaroon shouted at the two drivers.

The drivers immediately brought the chariot to a halt and Qaroon stepped out. He stared at the sycamore tree and slowly walked towards it. When he was under it, he looked around and started to remember everything that had taken place under the tree.

"Qaroon, go get Pharaoh before he gets us into trouble again." An echo of his father's voice passed through his mind. He then remembered himself chasing after a ram that was headed for the cornfield.

"Stay with your brothers, damned Pharaoh! Don't get us into trouble." An echo of his younger self passed through his mind.

"Damned Pharaoh!" Qaroon smiled.

He then looked at the ground and saw a rock. It was slightly browner than the rocks around it. It had dried blood on it.

"If you want to leave, then leave! But give me my share of this gold," he heard the memory of his father say.

"Your share? Of what?" Qaroon was having flashbacks of the last time he spoke to his father. He remembered as he pushed his father to stop him from taking the gold. He closed his eyes when he remembered the sound of his father's head hitting the rock.

Qaroon remembered his father's head bleeding out over the rock he was looking at.

"Stupid old man!" Qaroon muttered.

He then looked at the tree one more time, turned around, and started walking back towards the chariot.

Shortly after, the chariot was fast approaching Goshen. When it passed through the narrow roads of the village, children with dirty rags gathered around it. People came out of their huts and cottages wondering what the commotion could be.

"Who is that?" asked a bystander.

"Could it be the Pharaoh's chariot?" replied another.

"No Pharaoh would dare set his foot in our filthy village."

"Then could it be one of the Pharaoh's men?"

"Six horses? I doubt it!" The bystander dismissed the thought.

"Maybe they're here for Moses," whispered another.

One of the drivers got off the chariot and went to open the door. When Qaroon emerged, people were stunned. Not by who he was, but by what he was wearing. He had an Egyptian head covering that was decorated with all sorts of gems, his outfit was also encrusted with gems, he had a golden belt, golden bracelets, and golden necklaces, and his sandals were unlike any the people of Goshen had seen. They stared at Qaroon, who stood in front of them with pride and glamour. They whispered amongst themselves.

"Who is that?" a bystander whispered.

"He looks like Qaroon," another replied.

"Who is Qaroon?"

"The son of Izhar, the herdsman."

"We haven't seen him in years."

"I wish I had only a fraction of what he has!" said a third.

"What luck and good fortune transformed him from a sheep herdsman into such a wealthy man?"

"Why couldn't the rest of us have what he has?"

Qaroon looked around for a familiar face, but he didn't even have to try. Out of the entire crowd, none were as tall as his old preacher, Father Lawi. Qaroon walked to where father Lawi was standing. Father Lawi did not seem to react to Qaroon approaching. There was a young boy holding father Lawi's arm.

"The man from the chariot is coming in your direction, Father Lawi," said the boy.

"Hello there, Father Lawi!" Qaroon said.

Lawi's eyes were both white and he was not looking in Qaroon's direction.

"Is that you, son of Izhar?" he asked. He turned his head towards the source of Qaroon's voice.

"Yes, Father Lawi. I am Qaroon! "

Lawi turned to face the crowd. "Leave us now! I want to be alone with our guest."

Most people obeyed his order but some people stayed nearby to try to eavesdrop.

"Why have you returned, Qaroon?" Father Lawi asked in a disappointed tone.

"What do you mean?"

"After all that you've done to your people, how dare you show your face here?"

"What have I done, exactly?"

"We heard rumors a few months back. None of us believed them because we believed you were dead. And to be honest, those rumors sounded outrageous."

"What rumors?"

"Word came to the village that Adham, the owner of all the granaries in Egypt, the person who made us all suffer, was actually an Israelite named Qaroon. We didn't believe it was you until you showed up here in a chariot lead by six horses and dressed in an attire worthy of a Pharaoh."

Qaroon remained silent.

"So tell me, son of Izhar, why have you returned?" Lawi asked in stern tone.

"I am here to inspect my granary."

"Is that so?" Lawi said doubtfully. "Then why stop in the middle of the village dressed like that when the granary is outside of the village?"

"I came to see how my people are faring"

"Your people?" Lawi asked with disgust. "Your people are starving. Your people are being humiliated and tortured while you live in a fancy palace and impose your laws and thieving granaries upon them. Your people remain slaves to the Egyptians until this very day. But not for long!"

Qaroon smiled. "Are the brave people of Goshen finally going to take some action instead of sleeping in shit and getting humiliated by the Egyptians? Are they finally going to follow in my footsteps?" Qaroon laughed. "Tell me, Father Lawi, do you still preach in your disgusting hut? Are you finally telling the people of Goshen that they must fight back?"

"Laugh all you want, Qaroon! Our deliverer is finally here to liberate us from bondage and slavery, and also to liberate us from you and your granaries."

"Oh, I forgot that you were waiting for a deliverer! He's finally here? He's a few centuries late." Qaroon laughed again. "So who is this deliverer?"

"Moses, the son of Emran!"

"Moses?" Qaroon was surprised. "What was your God thinking? The man can hardly speak. He stutters too much. Merenptah will chop off his head before he even finishes the first sentence."

"Shame on you Qaroon! Don't mock God's prophet! He told us that he has met with God and talked to him. God sent both Moses and his brother, Aaron, to liberate us from Pharaoh and his tyranny."

"He spoke to God? Did God understand him or did God have to wait for a few days while Moses finished his sentences? Also, both of Emran's sons? You seriously believe that, Father Lawi? How do you know they're not lying? Did they bring proof that they were sent by God or that God exists at all?"

"We have faith in them!"

"Faith is an idiot's instrument of false hope! Instead of sleeping in shit like the rest of you and having faith that an invisible man in the sky will make things better for me, I went and made things better for myself without praying or begging. Everything I have achieved, I've achieved alone. Everything I have, I have acquired by my own hard work and sweat. While you sat here and begged your God for salvation, I was my own salvation. Not only did your God not answer any of your prayers, but he even made a fool out of you and made you blind! He didn't stop there, but your God went an extra step and sent you a stuttering man as a prophet." Qaroon laughed.

"You are a disrespectful and blasphemous man, Qaroon. God will punish you for all that you've done!" Lawi shouted.

"You said the same thing the last time you kicked me out of your disgusting hut. My slaves' residences are cleaner than your filthy house of God."

"The only reason you are where you are is because God has blessed you more than he blessed anyone. To test you and see what you will do with your fortune and the kind of decisions you will make."

"As I've told you before, old man, your God has done nothing for me! I've acquired all my wealth and possessions by my own knowledge and hard work. If he was truly the one who gave me, the blasphemous non-believer, this fortune, then why didn't he give you, the religious and devoted worshipper, the same fortune?" Qaroon asked.

"Don't be proud of what God gave you, Qaroon! God does not like proud people. There is a reason why God does what he does. There are reasons that we cannot comprehend. God is wise and knows all. He is the God of all mankind and not just the God of Israel," Lawi shouted.

"He is the God of weakness and humiliation! The God of slaves and beggars! The God of poverty and houses that smell like shit. I don't understand how you worship him when he has been most unkind to you and your people."

"Enough of this, Qaroon!" Lawi said in anger. "Tell me the real reason why you came back here!"

Qaroon was silent for a moment, but then he smiled. "I came to show off my fortune! To show you how much I am better than you! To show the people of Goshen how wrong they were to put their hope in a false God instead of working to earn their freedom like I did. To show them how wrong they were to submit to slavery and humiliation."

Lawi's expression turned to disgust. "It won't be long until they storm your gate, Qaroon! Those Egyptians, of whom you consider yourself to be a part… Once they all receive the news of you being an Israelite, they won't hesitate to burn you alive in your own palace. Because no matter how you dress, no matter how much gold you have, and no matter who you claim to be, you are still an Israelite. To them, you are no more than a slave who they would gladly kill for fun. Even your own slaves will not hesitate to do the same."

Qaroon's smile faded. He then turned around and started walking back towards his chariot.

"Son of Izhar! You are a slave!" Lawi shouted from a distance. "You may not look like one, you may not act like one, but you are more of a slave than any of us here." Lawi's voice started to fade away as Qaroon walked farther from him. "You are the worst kind of slave, Qaroon! You are a slave of your own making! A slave of your own possessions…"

Lawi's voice faded away when Qaroon reached his chariot. One of the drivers opened the door for him. He was just about to get inside.

"Qaroon!" yelled a woman's voice.

He looked behind the chariot, where two women were rushing towards him. One of them was old and slightly hunched while the other was holding the older woman's arm and was about Qaroon's age. He recognized them as his mother and sister Leah.

"Qaroon!" his mother called again.

When Qaroon and his mother's eyes met, the two of them stopped. He looked at his mother, who had teary eyes and was panting. He maintained a neutral expression while staring at them.

Qaroon stood still for a few moments staring at his mother and sister.

"Get us out of here!" He ordered the driver as he got into the chariot.

After the chariot door was closed, the driver whipped the horses and they started running.

"Qaroon!" his mother cried desperately and fell to her knees. "Qaroon!"

Her voice echoed in his ears and he teared up. He closed his eyes and a tear escaped and fell down his cheek. He reopened his eyes and his expression became grim.

A few days later, Qaroon sat on his long chair in his palace balcony. He was drinking wine from a bottle, while Ram, his slave, stood by his side waiting for orders.

"What are you looking at, you animal?" Qaroon shouted when he made eye contact with Ram.

"Nothing, master. I am just waiting for your orders," Ram said in a trembling voice.

"Go get me another bottle!" Qaroon shouted. "Now, slave!"

Ram rushed to get the bottle. He came back shortly and gave it to Qaroon.

"Did you see what those pigs did yesterday?" Qaroon asked.

Ram didn't reply but stood there terrified and stared at Qaroon.

"Those filthy slaves!" It was clear that Qaroon was drunk. "And you," Qaroon pointed at Ram. "I want you all out of my palace! Out!"

Ram was confused and didn't say a word.

"I said out!" Qaroon reached for a knife that was on the table next to his chair.

Ram panicked and started running away.

Qaroon started running after Ram. "I said out, you filthy slaves!" He tripped on a carpet and fell. He quickly got up and started chasing after Ram. When he arrived at the slaves' residence, the slaves were packing what they could and were running towards the exit of the palace.

"You filthy traitors! You would try to kill me? Your master?" Qaroon shouted as he walked towards them with the knife.

"Master Adham has gone mad!" a slave yelled.

"I am not a slave like the rest of you!" Qaroon was about to stab the slave that yelled but was struck on the head from behind. The last thing he heard was the sound of a vase breaking when it struck his head. Qaroon fell to the ground and was unconscious.

Qaroon woke up some time later. It was dark and he could barely see what was around him. He must have been unconscious for quite some time. He got up and heard himself stepping on what was left of the broken vase. He grabbed a nearby torch from its hanger on the wall and lit it. The fire shone light down the hallway. The slaves' residences were emptied out in a hurry. Qaroon stood still for a while, staring at the floor. He placed the torch back on the wall and took a piece of opium out of his pocket. He then sat down and started to chew on it.

A while later, Qaroon was still sitting in the same location, staring at the floor. He sighed.

"Master!" a man's voice echoed. It sounded familiar.

Qaroon looked around but saw no one. He then headed to where he thought the source of the voice came from.

"Master!" repeated the voice, a little louder.

Qaroon was getting closer to the source of the voice. It was coming from the basement. He grabbed a torch and opened the hidden door that lead down to the basement. He arrived in front of the first safe gate.

"Master!" the voice called from inside.

Qaroon set the torch aside and grabbed a massive key that unlocks the first gate. He struggled to open it but managed to do it after some effort. He then grabbed the torch and went inside.

"Master!" said the voice.

Qaroon turned to where the voice was coming from and saw Sharm, his former slave.

"Your orders, master!" Sharm said.

"What is this?" Qaroon asked in disgust. "What are you doing here? How can you be here?" Qaroon shouted. His voice echoed in the giant room.

Sharm faded away. Qaroon's eyes widened and he kept turning around in fear.

"Sharm!" Qaroon shouted.

Qaroon looked towards the second safe gate and there was blood flowing from under it. He set the torch aside and grabbed the key to the second safe. He opened the gate and went through. As soon as he was in, he was shocked to find two crocodiles feeding on the corpse of a man. Blood was leaking from his body towards the gate and there was a broken oar next to the man's corpse.

"Tomb raider!" the man said.

Qaroon watched as the man's corpse got ripped apart by the crocodiles.

He walked towards the third gate and opened it. When he entered, he smelled opium and could hear a man snoring. He turned to look behind the gate and saw Battari lying on the floor with a few empty bottles of wine next to him and a big piece of opium in his hand.

"I am... a God!" Battari slurred while snoring.

The snoring suddenly stopped and Qaroon heard a long exhale coming from Battari's mouth. That was the last breath he took. Qaroon looked at the fourth door and saw light coming from under it. He again set his torch aside and went ahead to open the fourth gate. When he went in, he had to cover his eyes because the flames inside the room were too bright. After getting adjusted to the brightness, he recognized the shape of a fat man inside the burning flame.

"How do you like your palace so far, great one?" asked the burning man. "It's unlike any I've ever built." The man started laughing.

He continued towards the fifth gate and opened it. Inside was the body of a man lying on the ground with his head bleeding out and an axe piercing through his rib cage. The man looked like he was struggling to say something.

"S…"

Qaroon came closer to hear what the man wanted to say.

"SS…" The man turned his head towards Qaroon. "Slave!"

Qaroon got shivers. He then opened the sixth gate and went through. He saw the blue corpse of a naked girl lying in the corner of the room facing the wall. She looked absolutely terrifying.

"What I do care about is those filthy animals getting what they deserve!" the girl said while turning her neck upwards to look at him.

"Qaroon!" a familiar voice called from beyond the seventh gate.

He walked over to the seventh gate and proceeded to open it. There was no one inside, only a massive rock in the center of the room.

It looked like one of the giant rocks that were inside the tomb that he and Minali were raiding. The sound of the rock grinding against the floor grew louder as it started to move.

"Qaroon!" Minali shouted faintly.

There was a hole under the rock. The more it moved, the louder Minali's voice got.

"Don't leave me in here, Qaroon! Please!" Minali cried.

The hole was just about uncovered. Minali's shouting was as loud as it could get.

"Qaroon!"

Once the hole was completely uncovered, Minali's yelling stopped. The room was dead silent again. Qaroon couldn't see anything inside the hole, but a smell of rotten corpses spread from the inside. Qaroon brought his torch above the hole to illuminate it. At the bottom was a body being chewed on by dozens of rats. Worms and bugs were crawling all over it. Qaroon looked upset. He got up and walked towards the eighth gate. When he entered, he smelled burning flesh.

"Water! I need water!"

The voice came from Benjamin, who was nailed to a cross with both his hands dripping blood and his chest full of lash marks and peeled skin. Qaroon's expression showed regret. He saw a bucket near the corner of the room so he walked over to it and submerged his hand in the water to fill the cup. When he turned around to return to Benjamin, he was gone. The water on Qaroon's hand turned red. He got startled and dropped the cup. Blood poured out of it and splashed on the floor. The cup disappeared, but the blood that was flowing on the floor remained and so did the blood on his hand. Qaroon teared up. He then heard the sound of a woman's crying. Qaroon proceeded to open the ninth gate. When he went in, he saw her lying down on her knees facing the tenth gate.

"Qaroon!" The woman cried and sniffed.

"Mother?" Qaroon started to tear up.

"Why wouldn't he want to see me?" she said, while tears ran down her cheeks.

Qaroon sat down next to her. "Mother, I'm sorry!" He cried.

She started to fade away. The last thing that remained of her were the echoes of her sobbing and sniffing, which quickly faded as well.

"Mother!" Qaroon cried loudly.

He sat on the ground for some time. He then got up and headed for the tenth gate. When he went in, he saw a man facing away from him to the other end of the room. The ninth gate closed behind him. The man was wearing peasant rags and a waist belt.

"Of course, who else could I possibly hallucinate?" Qaroon said sarcastically as he walked to stand next to the man.

"Good thing you killed less than ten people. Otherwise, we wouldn't all fit in your safes," Izhar said, laughing.

"You seem to be in a good mood for someone who was murdered by his own son," Qaroon said.

"I am a figment of your imagination, Qaroon! I imagine if the real Izhar were here, he would give you an earful."

Qaroon let out a faint smile "It's strange, I regret some of the things I did to some of the people across the gates, but I don't regret killing you."

"I know you don't. It's why your brain is making this interaction more pleasant than the others." Izhar smiled.

"So now what?" Qaroon asked.

"Now, you answer for your crimes."

"My crimes?"

"Yes, Qaroon! Your crimes."

"I'm not really in the mood," Qaroon said. He started walking back. "I'll come back later."

Qaroon walked back towards the ninth gate but it was shut. He tried to push it but it wouldn't move. The key was still on the other side.

Izhar turned around to face Qaroon. "Why did you kill Sharm?"

Qaroon was still trying to push the gate open.

"Why did I kill a backstabbing thief? You tell me!" Qaroon said. He turned around and walked towards Izhar. "He robbed me and betrayed my trust. He deserved it. Once I couldn't hypnotize him anymore, he was useless."

"Useless?" Izhar asked.

"I don't want my slave to think! I don't want him to get any ideas. I want him to stay sedated and harmless. If Sharm was aware of what he'd been doing for me, he would've smashed my head in long ago."

"Why not simply sell him? Why kill him?" Izhar asked.

"Betraying me has a price, and he paid it with his life."

"Why the boatman?"

"Are you going to ask me about all the people I've killed?" Qaroon asked in an angry tone. "You already know the answers to all your questions."

"I need to hear you say them. Just to make sure you're not fooling yourself."

"That filthy boatman deserved it. His curiosity is what got him killed. He could have just taken me to the other side of the river without searching through my bags, but he couldn't resist. Only one of us was going to get off that boat alive. I made sure it was me."

"How do you know the boatman would have killed you? He might have let you go for a piece of gold or two."

"Because people are envious by nature. If he couldn't have it, he would've made sure that I didn't have it either. I would have been damned if I gave him any of it willingly."

"Why Battari? He posed no threat to you! You could've left him sleeping and made off with the gold."

"He knew who I was. He knew what I looked like. I couldn't just let him live. Had he done his job properly instead of lusting after wine and opium, maybe he would still be alive."

"But why Hoor?"

"He was a liability. He was the only other living person who knew where all my treasures would be placed."

"No other reasons?" Izhar asked doubtfully.

"That reason alone was more than good enough for me to get rid of him. But it's not the only reason." Qaroon paused. "When I started all of this, my goal was to be better than anyone in Goshen. Better than the whole of Israel. That was ridiculously easy to achieve because any man with more than three cows can easily pass as the richest man in Goshen. So I aimed a bit higher and wanted to be better than all the Egyptians. I had to be what they weren't and I had to have what they didn't. Hoor threatened to make them all my equals by making them similar palaces. He even told me he could make better ones," Qaroon shouted. "I couldn't have that. One push was all it took to guarantee the safety of my superiority over the Egyptians."

"How about the Egyptian farmer whom you killed with the axe?" Izhar asked.

"It was definitely not because of a stupid ball," Qaroon said. "The way he spoke to me, it was like he was speaking to a lesser creature—an animal! Killing him proved to me that not only am I his equal, but that I am superior." He paused for a few moments. "People like him are what are wrong with the world. People like him are the reason Egyptians enslaved the Israelites. People like him are everywhere. I had a choice: I could either become like them or I could become like you," he said, giving his father a disgusted look. "I could either become a master or remain a slave. I could either rebel against my fate or accept it."

"I'm assuming you killed his daughter for the same reason?"

"Egyptians will not learn that we are their equals on their own. They need to learn it by force. Blood needs to be shed! Their women need to be raped and their children need to be killed! We need to do to them exactly what they do to us. We need to force them to understand that they are not our superiors. Then, and only then, can we be free of this plague."

"Such a good speech, Qaroon! Have you considered taking Father Lawi's place?" Izhar smiled.

Qaroon shook his head. "The people of Israel do not want to be saved. They are satisfied with their lives. I don't plan to waste my time trying to convince a chained up man that his key to freedom is within arm's reach. He already knows that. He simply refuses to reach for the key."

"I won't ask you why you killed Minali. I will, however, ask you why you killed him in such a horrible way."

"Like the others, Minali was a necessary sacrifice. He was a liability and had to die."

"Minali was trapped in a pitch black tomb that smelled like a century old corpse. The only things he could hear other than the sound of his own breathing were the footsteps of rats. All he had was the piece of opium that you gave him. He was probably alive in that room for a few days. So I ask you this, why not just stab him or smash his skull with a rock? Why make him die such a horrifying death?" Izhar asked.

Qaroon was quiet for a few moments. "Minali wasn't like the other Egyptians. He was kind and gullible, naive and foolish. I will admit that I do regret what I did to him. Not a day goes by where I don't hear his final echoes in my mind. But if I had to do it again, I would. I would bury alive as many people as necessary. But I still felt guilty. Trying to marry his sister was a way of clearing my conscience."

Izhar paused for a few moments and then turned to face Qaroon.

"Do you consider yourself to be an evil man, Qaroon?"

"No." He paused. "But I have to be! I have to be as brutal and as inhumane as the Egyptians if I am to compete with them. I have to be merciless. A good man has no place in this world except under the feet of others who will try to use him. Life today forces people to be greedy and only think about themselves. If they show kindness or selflessness or any sign of weakness, they will get stepped on and crushed. Yes, I have some regrets, but in the end, it is all a matter of crushing or being crushed. I would rather others suffer instead of me. Simple as that."

"But nothing you did could ever come close to what you did to Benjamin," Izhar said in a disappointed tone.

Qaroon did not reply but started to tear up.

"Did he deserve it?" Izhar asked.

"He was my only friend. The one person I trusted. For me, it's impossible to trust people, and he betrayed that trust."

"Did he deserve it?" Izhar demanded.

"Yes!" Qaroon shouted. "But I didn't mean to set him on fire. At first, I wanted to, but I couldn't. All of this happened because I was weak. I thought I could trust him so I made him the manager of the gold mine. I gave him the opportunity to use me and step on my back. And he did! I almost died because I was weak and I trusted someone other than myself. So yes, he deserved it."

Izhar did not reply but shook his head.

"You think you're any better than I am?" Qaroon asked angrily. "You think you're a moral man? What you did was far worse than what I did."

"Is that so?" Izhar asked.

"You watched your family and people be tortured, raped, and killed, and you did nothing. You watched as everyone you knew was humiliated and have their dignity taken away and you did nothing. Is that moral? I have felt more sympathy and regret for the people I've killed than you have for your own daughter when she was raped in front of you. Did your conscience tell you that it is right to let your children suffer? Did your conscience tell you that it is right to sit down and beg God for help instead of taking action? Taking action was the moral decision. What I did was right."

"I have made mistakes in my life, Qaroon. What man doesn't? What man doesn't sin? A man can come back from his mistakes. A damaged conscience can never be fully repaired, but it is always trying to heal."

"Having a conscience makes a man weak. And a weak man has no place in this world."

They were both silent for a few moments.

"Why didn't you go to her?" Izhar asked in a sad tone.

Qaroon was silent for a few moments and his eyes teared up. "I couldn't... I couldn't face her. After everything I've done... I couldn't... I wanted to, but I couldn't." Qaroon cried.

"She was down on her knees, Qaroon! Crying! Why didn't you go to her?" Izhar asked in a stern tone.

"Because I miss her!" Qaroon shouted. "I miss her and my sisters. I miss my miserable life in that pile of donkey shit. I had nothing back there, but I was happier than I am now. Now I have everything I could possibly dream of, yet I am more miserable than I ever was before," Qaroon cried. "But what did that mean? How could I explain that feeling? I have gold and riches beyond imagination. The keys to my safes make even the strongest man struggle to carry them. I have a palace fit for a Pharaoh, and I still miss that filthy village of slaves. I even went back there to show off my riches to them so I could feel better about myself, but it didn't work. I still missed Goshen," Qaroon cried. "My feelings had to be wrong. There was no way that it made sense that I would leave all of this and all of what I have achieved and run back to that God-forsaken village. So I got in the chariot. I decided to bury those false feelings and move on. If I had shown any sign of weakness, I would have ended up hugging her and my sister," Qaroon said. A tear escaped his eye.

"Perhaps weakness isn't such a bad thing, son. Maybe the world needs a bit of weakness. Maybe when we are all weak, we will help each other become stronger. But the problem is that people only think of themselves and place their own interest above that of others. People love themselves a bit too much, which many think is completely fine and natural. People refuse to be weak because they fear that their fellow man will step on them and crush them. If weakness is what it takes to make us rely on one another and trust one another, then I say we give it a chance. Maybe then, Israelites and Egyptians can unite and join forces. Maybe then can they start treating each other like human beings instead of objects or tools that they can use to make themselves stronger. One strong man alone is weak; but many weak men together are strong."

"What you propose is impossible to achieve. People are infested with greed and self-love, and they will never grow above it or change. It is their nature. The Israelites, however weak, will never stand together because they all fear for their lives; and the Egyptians, however strong, will never stand together because they fear for their lives and possessions. This is how things are and this is how things will always be. You may find some selfless and sacrificing people, but their efforts will always be ruined by people like me. It's too late for humanity to change."

"It's never too late for humanity to change, Qaroon. But it is too late for you."

The ground started shaking.

"What is this?" Qaroon asked.

"It is time, son!"

The ground started shaking more violently. The floor under the well cracked open and the well fell into the crack. The boxes that were stacked in the room started falling and the gold pieces that were in them scattered all over the room. Hundreds of boxes released tens of thousands of pieces of gold and jewelry. The ceiling from above Qaroon started to collapse and rubble started falling down in pieces.

"God! If I make it out of here alive, I'll change!" Qaroon shouted. "I'll be your most loyal servant."

"It's too late for that, Qaroon!" Izhar said as he started to fade away.

After Izhar disappeared, Qaroon watched as the floor around him started opening up in multiple areas. The gold was still pouring out of the falling boxes and was rolling towards the center of the room. He was right in the center, so he had thousands of pieces of gold pile up around his feet and up to his ankles. He looked up and saw the roof of the basement crack open and reveal the ceiling of his palace. Qaroon felt that he was descending. It was as if the ground under the palace had cracked open and was in the process of swallowing the palace.

"Is this all you can come up with? An earthquake?" Qaroon shouted.

The palace was still descending into the ground. The palace ceiling cracked open and he got a glimpse of the blue sky. Hundreds of birds were flying over the palace. Qaroon heard the sound of water splashing nearby. The palace kept descending until it was below the level of the nearby lake. The palace ceiling kept falling apart and getting wider until water started rushing in from the top. Qaroon watched in horror as a massive wave of water made its way down at a remarkable speed and reached the bottom of the basement. The wave that formed upon impact pushed him off his feet and forced him along with it. The wave pushed Qaroon towards a nearby pillar. His head hit the pillar and he was knocked unconscious. Water from the lake kept pouring in until eventually the palace was flooded with water. Qaroon's unconscious body was moving along with the waves as they gradually calmed down. Once the waves settled, his body started falling to the bottom. Qaroon slowly fell on a massive pile of gold. He opened his eyes and watched how his entire palace and fortune were now submerged under water and were in the process of being swallowed by the earth. Qaroon started to choke. He grabbed a handful of gold pieces and looked at them in disgust. The basement was getting darker as the palace was further underground. The earth stopped shaking, the waters calmed down, and Qaroon's hand let go of the pieces of gold, which slowly fell towards the ground.

Sometime later, on a hot summer day, the sky was blue with no clouds. Two farmers could be seen ploughing a piece of land and three children were running around nearby and playing with a ball made of straw and pine tree leaves. An old man was walking towards a fruitful sycamore tree. He had white hair, a white beard, and was hunching. He was wearing peasant rags and had a walking stick. After the man reached the base of the tree, he sat down slowly and exhaled. He sat there in the shade for some time until one of the three children ran up to him.

"Grandfather Helal! It's time for us to go back! Mother is waiting!"

"Really?" asked Helal with a smile. "This soon? Are you and your cousins done playing, Minali?"

"No, but father said it's time to go."

"So your father and your uncle Basmi are done ploughing the land?"

"Yes, Grandfather!"

"Very well! Will you help your old grandfather up?" Helal asked. He extended his hand towards his grandson, Minali.

The child grabbed Helal's hand and tried to pull him up. "You're too heavy for me!"

Helal laughed and got up slowly. "So there's no chance of you carrying me to the donkeys?" he asked playfully. "I'm too old to be walking."

"Will you pay me?" the child asked with a smile.

Helal laughed. "You remind me of your uncle Minali! He always asked for gold for his services. He'd even ask for gold when I asked him to get me water." Helal's smile became faint and his eyes teared up.

"When am I going to meet uncle Minali?" the child asked.

"I honestly don't know. I haven't seen him in very a long time."

They both started walking towards the donkeys.

"Why was I named after him?" Minali asked.

"Your father Daniali and your uncle Minali were inseparable when they were children. Your father loved his brother so much that he decided to name his son after him."

Helal and his grandson arrived to where Daniali, Basmi, and Basmi's two sons were waiting. They had three donkeys packed and ready to go.

"I'm glad you finished early today, boys!" said Helal while looking at Daniali and Basmi. "Any longer and your old man would have passed out or burned in the sun." He smiled.

"Nonsense, father Helal!" said Basmi. "You're in excellent shape for a man your age." He smiled.

"Hypocrisy!" Helal smiled. "You're just saying these things because I let you marry my daughter."

Basmi helped Helal get up on a donkey. He then helped one of his sons up on the same donkey in front of Helal. He got on a donkey with his other son. Minali rode with his father, Daniali. They drove the donkeys forward and were on their way home.

Back at Helal's house, they sat around a platform with wooden plates in front of them. There were four extra plates set on the platform. Lamia came in with Daniali's wife carrying food dishes. Two more girls walked in carrying cups of water and a plate of bread. The family sat down around the platform and started to eat.

"Grandfather!" said one of the girls. "Why don't we have slaves? My friend Sati at the nearby farm told me her father owns two slaves who help him around his farm."

"Very good question, Samia!" Helal said with a smile. "Slaves are people, my dear, like you and me! They don't deserve to be treated like that. Tell me, children, would any of you like it if you became slaves? Would you be fine if someone chained you up and took away your freedom?"

The children shook their heads.

"Then why own a slave if you're not fine with being one yourself? Why rob someone of their freedom if you cherish your own?" Helal paused to take a bite of bread. "Today, Egyptians treat their farm animals and dogs better than they treat their slaves. They treat animals better than they treat their own kind. When a man loses his cow or mule, he feels loss, grief, and sorrow. But when thousands of people of his own kind die, not even a single tear is shed. Can any of you tell me why?" Helal asked.

Helal's grandchildren all shook their heads.

"It's because of greed!" said Helal. "Greed is what makes us love ourselves so much and makes us was to enrich and empower ourselves at the expense of others. Greed is what makes us never settle for what we have but always strive for more. And greed is what makes us love possessions. Mankind is cursed with an uncontrollable love of possessions."

Helel paused for a moment and looked at his family members, who were eating and looking at him.

"It was never enough! No matter how much wealth we had, it was simply never enough. We had to have more. So we made the lives of our fellow man into a possession that we can praise as a luxury. Our greed has gotten out of control." Helal took a sip of water from his cup.

"But isn't greed natural, Grandfather?" asked one of the children.

"Yes, it is!" Helal nodded. "But the kind of greed we see today is unnatural. Greed is meant to coexist with all the other traits and emotions that we have, but greed has outgrown them all. People seem to believe that true happiness lies in their possessions; that the whole purpose of life is to acquire as many objects and materials as possible. But there is one thing that everyone forgets: these possessions do us no good at our deathbeds. These possessions do not prolong our lives or stop our deaths."

"But we need these possessions in the afterlife," said Basmi's older son. "People who are richer fare better in the afterlife. People like Qaroon, for example, will have the best afterlife possible. So their lives were not really wasted."

"Who is Qaroon?" asked Minali.

"Qaroon was a slave who became the wealthiest man in Egypt," replied Helal. "He had gold and riches beyond imagination. Some say he was so rich that his fortune could last him a thousand lifetimes."

"What happened to him?" asked Minali.

"One day, the earth swallowed him and his palace whole and he drowned next to his fortune. After the incident, people named the lake that drowned him 'Qaroon's Lake.'"

"He's going to have a better afterlife than anyone. When he wakes up and finds all of his gold and fortune waiting for him in the afterlife, he's going to be so happy," said Minali.

"I don't think so!" said Helal. "Tell me, Minali, do you hear the stories of tomb raiders who rob the tombs of the Pharaohs?"

"Yes!" replied Minali.

"How come their gold is still there? They've been dead for centuries. They should be in their afterlife by now. Why is their gold still here? And why is it still being stolen by the living?"

Minali did not reply but only shrugged his shoulders.

"I imagine that if Qaroon's palace was ever found, all of his possessions would still be there, untouched. The only thing missing would be Qaroon himself. Sure, his body, or what remains of it, will be there, but not his spirit. Qaroon has moved on and has left his treasure behind. My point is that, yes, there may be an afterlife, but there is no place for worldly possessions there."

"If we don't have possessions, then what do we have in the afterlife?" Samia asked.

"It is called the judgement of the dead for a reason. It doesn't make sense for them to judge us based on how much wealth we've acquired, because then only the rich would prosper in the so-called afterlife and the rest of us would be left with nothing. The only things we have in the afterlife are things that cannot be stolen. Things that last and can never be taken away. They are the memories that we make. The lasting impressions we leave on people and the kind of relationships we have with them. The decisions and many choices that we make. Those things we take with us to the afterlife. Take Qaroon for example. He spent his entire life pursuing wealth and power. He allowed greed to consume him and he used every person in front of him as a stepping stone to raise himself higher. Yes, he had riches beyond imagination, but what good did that do him? In the end, he suffered a horrible death alone, without a friend or loved one. The memory of Qaroon on this earth is a vile and evil one, consumed by greed. He has not done a single act of kindness towards anyone other than himself. No one can recall a good memory of Qaroon. Do you really think gold and silver can make up for that? Does it make sense that riches and possessions vouch for a man's character? Maybe in this world, but certainly not in the next. He now stands before the Gods empty handed, with only a memory of his possessions. Nothing more!" Helal paused to drink some water.

He looked at all his family members, who were all staring at him. He smiled.

"I am happy!" He teared up. "I have all of you here with me. I love you all so dearly, and knowing that you all love me makes me have so much more than Qaroon ever did. I am old and I don't have much time left, but I want you all to know: I am happy!"